MW01635951

IN TOO DEEP

To Lorraine

IN TOO DEEP

•

Terri Alcock

Best Wishes
Terri Alcock

AVALON BOOKS
NEW YORK

Library of Congress Catalog Card Number: 00-102194
ISBN 0-8034-9439-4

All the characters in this book are fictitious,
and any resemblance to actual persons,
living or dead, is purely coincidental.
Published by Thomas Bouregy & Co., Inc.
160 Madison Avenue, New York, NY 10016

PRINTED IN THE UNITED STATES OF AMERICA
ON ACID-FREE PAPER
BY HADDON CRAFTSMEN, BLOOMSBURG, PENNSYLVANIA

For Doug, who told me, when my first book was published that
he had always wanted to write a mystery.
This one's for you!
And for my nephew, David, who dreams of becoming
a famous writer. Follow your dreams and they become reality!

Chapter One

I can't believe Bill's latest idea! My old buddy, Bill Henry, former high school friend and confidant, is retiring from the police force to open a private detective agency and he wants me as his partner. Me—a P.I.! When he first broached the subject, I laughed out loud, told him to get a grip, and continued eating my lunch. Bill works plainclothes detail with Victoria's finest. When he called me out of the blue and asked me to meet him I said yes, thinking nothing of it. I figured he wanted to discuss our mutual friend, Emily. She was *my* friend, but of late, Bill's seeing more of her than me.

He never mentioned Emily. He was waiting when I arrived at the restaurant, having suggested we skip The Purple Cabbage, my usual hangout, and meet at Barnaby's, a local steak house. Bill knows I'm a reluctant vegetarian who falls off the wagon at every opportunity. When I opened the door, I spotted him ensconced in the corner booth. From the look of the bread basket, he'd already sampled the crusty French loaf.

"I ordered two T-bone steaks with fried potatoes—heavy on the fat, light on the salad," he greeted me.

The food arrived soon after me, and we dug in, hardly taking time to exchange the usual pleasantries. He waited till I was so full I could hardly push myself back from the table, then sprung his idea.

"Sam, you've always said you want to get out of the rat race and spend more time writing. Were you serious?"

"Yeah, of course," I said, eyebrows forming a question as I continued to force down one final bite with the hand that held the fork and undid the button on my jeans with the other.

What the heck did Bill have up his sleeve? I should have known there was a price tag attached to every deliciously tender morsel of steak.

"I've got a great idea!" Bill said, pausing while I laid down my fork and looked regretfully at my empty plate. Satisfied he had my full attention, he continued, "You know how well we work together."

"We do?" Skepticism must have been pasted on my face because he launched into a very convincing argument.

"Look at that little skirmish a couple of months ago." He was referring to a recent mess I'd poked my nose into. I'd gone running to him for help when things threatened to get sticky.

"I'll concede your assistance was invaluable, Bill, but that doesn't prove anything."

"Look," he insisted, "you've got a nose for investigation and I've got police experience. I've been thinking of quitting the force for quite a while. I've put in enough years to get a decent pension when I retire."

He hesitated and looked around the restaurant as though convinced the other patrons were spying for a foreign power.

"I've been thinking about marriage again," he admitted in a tone that indicated his reluctance to broadcast the information to a wider audience. As if his feelings for Emily were top secret!

Nevertheless, I was a bit surprised at his declaration. He and Emily *had* been spending a lot of time together but I didn't know they had progressed to talk of marriage.

He continued, "I don't want to make the same mistakes with Emily that I made the first time around."

"So, what's that got to do with me, Bill?"

"You'd like to be your own boss, wouldn't you, Sam? Have more time to write book number three?" he wheedled, hitting a vulnerable spot. "If we were working together, you'd be able to do that. We'd make a great team as Hope and Henry, P.I.s. You're organized, with good computer skills, and you have an insatiable curiosity. I've got credibility, experience, and contacts in the business community. We could start small, take on a few insurance investigations, the occasional divorce, just to get going, and branch out from there. You're not hurting for money, Sam, your last book did quite well. This might be an opportune time to take the plunge. What do you say?" Finishing his sales pitch, he sat back and waited.

You could have knocked me over with a feather. Never in a million years had I considered the possibility of being paid to snoop—something that came as naturally to me as breathing. What a concept!

"I don't know Bill," I said, frowning slightly, but he knew, and I knew, he had me hooked. I was already picturing our names in big, gold letters on the door of a very posh office.

By the way, I'm Samantha Hope, better known to family and friends as Sam. At thirty-six, you'd think I'd know better, but each and every day I battle an overactive imagination, more curiosity than the proverbial cat, and a knack for getting into trouble.

I live with my roommate and friend, Gabrielle Bernard, and our two Old English sheepdogs, Clem and Mimi. Gabby and I are more like sisters really. We met at dog obedience class. The fact that we both had Old English sheepdogs seemed serendipitous enough that we started hanging out together, taking the dogs for walks and so on. Since neither of us had a love interest at the time—me having gone through a rather unpleasant divorce and Gabby suffering from a severe case of unrequited love—we decided to pool our resources and buy an apartment together. We have our squabbles, like real sisters, but on the whole get along pretty well, having a healthy respect for each other's space and yet enjoying each other's company.

Our apartment is located in the Banana Belt off Canada's West Coast. It forms part of a stately old character home in James Bay, an eclectic neighborhood in the heart of Victoria, the province's capital. Victoria is renowned for afternoon tea, bagpipes and kilts, and dangerous gray-haired grannies on scooters who'll run you down at the least excuse.

The apartment is a stone's throw from the Provincial Legislative Buildings, which would have been handy in my younger, more radical days. Now it just means streets overrun with gawking tourists all summer, but a minor inconvenience considering the advantages of the location. We're close to Beacon Hill Park, shopping and theaters and breathtaking views of the ocean and harbor.

We lead a quiet life. Our main recreation is walking the beaches with the dogs or playing bridge with friends. Gabby seems satisfied to live this rather staid existence, but there are times when I crave excitement. My snooping provides a relatively harmless outlet. Most of the time.

Bill's right about one thing. I have a perfectly good job doing research for a consulting firm. But somehow it just doesn't satisfy me. I want to write and am continually frustrated by the lack of time to sink my teeth into my writing. Even with two mystery novels under my belt, I still dream of giving birth to the Great Canadian Novel. If I wasn't reporting to an office every morning, there'd be more time to waste at the computer.

He's right about the money angle, too. I'm not rich, but the apartment's almost paid for and my books, though they haven't allowed me to quit my day job, have enabled me to set aside a little for a rainy day.

"I'll give you a week to think about it," Bill interrupted my rambling thoughts, "then I want a decision. Go home and mull it over. I'll talk to Emily. We'll meet again a week from today. If the answer's yes, I'll pay again—to celebrate. If it's no, it'll be your treat!" Bill grabbed the check, threw a tip on the table, and we headed to the exit.

Walking back to the office, I looked up at the stark gray cement building I'd called home every day from nine to five, not including overtime, for the past several years. It dominated the skyline, with its tinted windows that wouldn't open and uniformed security at the door.

If I took Bill up on his offer, what would I be giving up? Easy—a regular paycheck. Gabby might have something to say about that since it might mean I'd be a little short on my share of expenses from time to time. What else? I couldn't think of a single thing. Sure, I'd miss some of the people I worked with, but those who'd become friends would continue to be and the others came and went. Certainly, I wouldn't miss the hours, the tight deadlines, the rules and regulations.

What would I be gaining? That was easier—a chance to spend time indulging in my favorite sport—snooping into other people's business. Admittedly, this predilection got me into a heap of trouble at times, but so far I'd always wiggled out unscathed.

Bill had blown me away with his offer. He's an unrepentant chauvinist, normally only capable of accepting women in traditional roles. Now he wanted to go into business with me and to top it off, in spite of disapproving loudly of my snooping in the past, he'd suggested we do it for a living.

Bill and I went back a long way. We'd kept in touch over the years, crying on each other's shoulder when suffering from a broken heart, using each other as convenient dates, knowing it was safe to do so, since there wasn't even a hint of romance between us. If, and this is a big if, I *were* going to fall for any guy, he'd be the type to make my heart beat faster, though. Tall, dark, and handsome, like a tacky hero in a drugstore romance, he sports a cute little mustache and has short wavy hair. He works out and keeps himself in great shape.

He's been a cop for close to twenty years. I hadn't known he was thinking of quitting the force, but it made sense. Emily was his first serious romantic involvement since his ex-wife, Margaret. He'd seen the writing on the wall; Emily wasn't used to sitting home alone. No way she'd take herself out of circulation for someone who was never around. She'd definitely approve of his plan to quit the force and set himself up as a private investigator.

I wondered how Gabby would react to this latest harebrained scheme. Though it was obviously my decision, I valued her opinion. I already knew I wanted to take Bill up on his offer, but it would be nice if she agreed since whatever I was involved in affected her as well.

On my way home from work, I stopped at the Birdcage Confectionery, the oldest corner store in Victoria, and picked out a bouquet of flowers. Although the January weather was a little chilly, orchids, chrysanthemums, and other blossoms whose names escape me, if I ever knew them, bloomed in buckets outside the store. I settled on a spray of beautiful purple and turquoise orchids. They were so vivid that they looked as if they were spray-painted by some budding artist.

Gabby would love them. Purple is a very spiritual color according to her, and she should know. She's into all that metaphysical gobbledygook: meditation, auras, colors, and crystals. For the life of me, I can't understand why any rational person would want to complicate life on this plane by trying to travel to others. But I keep my mouth shut most of the time, unless she and some of her Psychic Circle try to include me in their activities. "Live and let go," that's my motto.

The dogs came bounding from the kitchen to greet me when I let myself into the house. Their pleasure at seeing me arrive home after work was still gratifying even after a couple of years of the same routine. I rewarded them with biscuits and went into the kitchen where Gabby was stirring a pot on the stove.

"Sam, what have you been up to? You look like you've got something big on your mind."

"What do you mean?"

How did she do that? She always seemed to know when something was up. She turned her attention back to the concoction on the stove.

"What's for dinner?" I'm lousy in the kitchen but Gabby's great. We have a deal. She cooks and I clean up the mess. We eat well even though it's vegetarian fare. And if I slip out for a hamburger or steak once in a while, where's the harm in it?

"Curried vegetables and rice. But it won't be ready for a while. Why don't you pour us a glass of wine?

"Red or white?" This is something I've never figured out. If you're not eating meat, how do you know which wine to serve with dinner? One of life's little mysteries, I guess.

"I'll have white; there's some chilling in the fridge."

I poured two glasses, and we took them into the living room. *Well, here goes nothing,* I thought, as I prepared to give my sales pitch. She had always been a little wary of my snooping—worried I might stumble into a hornet's nest.

"Gabby, there's something I want to get your advice on."

"I knew it!" she hollered. "I knew something was up. So my intuition is still working! That's reassuring."

"Seriously, I just want to tell you about my lunch date with Bill."

"Shoot. What's with Bill? Is he still gaga over Emily? We haven't seen them in a while."

"I'll tell him you said that," I snickered, stalling for time. "Actually, we didn't discuss Emily." I took another sip of wine and held the glass up to the light, examining it like a professional vintner. That killed a few more minutes. Then I carefully put down the glass.

"He wanted to talk about a career change."

"Really?" Gabby was puzzled. "Is Bill thinking about getting out of police work?"

"He is, actually, but I was talking about *me,* not him."

"Why the sudden interest in your career?" Gabby studied me from behind her wineglass.

"He's thinking of quitting the force to set up his own private investigation company. It would leave him more time for Emily. He'd be able to set his own hours and take on as much or as little work as he wanted. They're getting quite serious."

"Uh-oh, I can see where this is heading." She sat back, her arms folded stiffly across her chest.

"Hold on," I interjected. "Let me finish before you go shooting me down. Bill knows I'm fed up with work. He's heard my endless whining about wanting to win the lottery or make a killing with one of my books so I can quit work. He's come up with a brilliant idea. *He* thinks we should go into business together. 'Hope and Henry, P.I.s'. What do you think?" I mumbled the last part, hoping that by making it less audible the idea would be more palatable.

"Let me get this straight. You want to quit your job and become a private investigator?" The look on her face was priceless, a mixture of amusement and incredulity. She started to laugh. "You're joking, right?"

"I've never been more serious." If only there were some way to make the idea sound less half-baked and more legit. "I would never have thought of it myself, but now that Bill has, I can see how perfect it could be. You know how I like digging into things."

"Or digging them up," she said sarcastically, referring to a recent escapade.

"Gabby, listen, I know this sounds like another of my crazy schemes, but don't you think it might be worth a try? I've got a few bucks in the bank. I'd like to try it for a year. If it doesn't work out, or if I can't make a decent living between working with Bill and selling my writing, I'll go back to my dull, boring, horrible job and never mention it again."

She sat quietly for a few moments before speaking. "If it's that important to you, Sam, then I have to say go for it. Otherwise you'll always wonder if it would have worked out."

I jumped up and gave her a big hug, almost knocking over the coffee table in the process.

"Give me your solemn word that you'll keep Bill and me in the loop. Promise you'll tell us everything so we don't have to worry about what we don't know in addition to what we do."

She had a point. I was accustomed to operating solo, and had never rid myself of the habit of making decisions and acting on them without consulting anyone. I'd never been a good team player. But there was a good explanation for my behavior: some of my crazy projects would be discouraged before they got off the ground if I told anyone in advance.

I had learned early to keep my plans to myself. When I was growing up, my older sister Martha had always given her opinion and advice whether or not it was sought.

Take the whole business of my father. He and I have recently been reunited. I hadn't even known he existed until a short while ago. For years, Martha and my mother had hidden the fact that the man I thought was my father was actually my mother's second husband and our stepfather. Mother had divorced our father when I was two and remarried soon after. No one bothered to tell me. During my teens I found this out quite by accident. But because of my mother's pleas, I'd waited until last year to begin searching for my birth father. When Martha and Mother found out I'd located him, they were livid. Ever since that time, I'd been trying to convince Martha to get reacquainted with Father. He really wanted it and so did I.

"I promise, I swear on my life that I will tell you everything. This is going to be so fantastic, Gabby."

"So you say." She smiled. "I'm not convinced, but give it a try anyway. Give it a year, then take stock. By then you should know if it's really what you want."

And that's how I got two free steak dinners out of Bill in less than a week.

Chapter Two

Once the decision was made, it was only a couple of months before Bill and I were standing outside our new office, admiring our names on the door. Getting the agency up and running was left to me while Bill finished up his police work and prepared to leave the force. I found us a great location on the third floor of a small office building in the James Bay commercial center. There were three rooms—a reception area and two offices—the larger one was for Bill and the smaller one for me. Mine had a view of the ocean, if you didn't mind standing on a chair to peer out the high window.

We each furnished our own space, and Emily decorated the reception area. Gabby hooked up our computers and set up idiot-proof systems for tracking files and keeping appointments straight. It all came together for me when a sign painter had lettered our names in gold: *"Hope & Henry,"* and underneath, *"Private Investigators"* on our front door. It was just as I'd envisioned back in January when Bill had presented the idea. We were finally in business. Now all we needed were clients.

We agreed that, until we got busy, I'd use the office to write in the mornings so I could be on hand to answer the phone. Bill would get out and hustle, making contacts and drumming up business. We had business cards printed, gave them out to all our friends, and put a discreet advertisement in the classified section of the local newspaper.

I gave my notice at work, and they had a party for me, giving me a magnifying glass and toy pistol as a joke, then presenting me with a beautiful leather briefcase. I left with few regrets.

Monday, the third of March, was our first day on the new job. I hollered good-bye to Gabby who was working in her office upstairs, saying I'd see her at noon, then walked briskly to the office, which was only five minutes away.

I'd decided to take Mimi along to keep me company, so she walked beside me. Though she still acted like an over-exuberant puppy, her behavior had improved over the winter so I thought she could stay out of trouble. The younger of the two dogs, she had attached herself to me as if I was her mother. Mimi and I had bonded from day one and were constant companions.

I let myself into the office and hung up my jacket, checking the answering machine on my way past the reception area. Bill and I were supposed to share office duties until we could afford secretarial help, but knowing Bill as I did, if I wasn't careful I'd find myself acting as his receptionist.

A note on my desk said, "*Meet me at the coffee shop across the street at one—Bill.*" Coffee. Good idea! I put a pot on to brew and ran down to the store to pick up cream. The coffee was steaming hot and aromatic when I returned. Pouring myself a cup, I sat down at my desk, put my feet up, and looked around. I couldn't get the silly grin off my face. I was as happy as a clam.

Turning on the radio, I hummed along as I worked, organizing some rough notes for my third book, which was in the preliminary stages. I took all my scribbling, written on napkins and torn bits of paper, and transferred them to the computer. Then I worked on developing character profiles and wrote a letter to my publisher proposing a date when a first draft of the manuscript could be ready.

The telephone rang once. I answered, "Hope and Henry, good morning." It was a wrong number. Never mind, it wouldn't be long until the phone would be ringing off the hook. *Enjoy the peace and quiet while it lasts, Sam,* I thought.

At noon, Mimi and I walked home. Gabby had been out all morning and hadn't had time to prepare lunch, so we worked together to mix up a salad and open a can of soup.

"How was your first morning on the job, Sam?"

"Wonderful," I gloated. "I love this, working on my own."

"What about Bill?" Gabby asked between spoonfuls of soup.

"He was out all morning; just Mimi and I holding down the fort, right Mimi?" Mimi's ears perked. "I'm meeting him at one."

"Any calls, any prospects?"

"Just one call—a wrong number. But it'll happen. It takes time to establish any new business."

"Well, I have to get back to work." Gabby got up from the table. "I'm assembling a computer system for that new electronics firm on Yates Street."

"That's quite a feather in your cap. Say! Maybe you can take some of our business cards and drop them off wherever you go." I fished a handful out of my briefcase and handed them to her.

"Gotta run. See you later." She dashed off, and I cleaned up the dishes then walked back in the direction of the office.

The Coffee Connection was situated diagonally from the office and Bill was sitting on one of the high stools at the counter in front of the window, reading the newspaper. He looked up and waved as I walked in.

"Hi, Sam. How was your first morning at the office?"

"Quiet and wonderful! Where were you?" I plunked myself down next to him, after ordering a cappuccino.

"Went to see Stan Prescott. I guess you could say he's a rival, since he's a P.I. He works alone. We used to walk a beat together years ago. You might remember him?" He paused to take a sip of his coffee.

I nodded. I recalled having heard Bill mention Stan's name.

"He's got more work than he can handle right now, said he'd be willing to throw some our way for a finder's fee. What do you think? Just till we start getting some clients of our own?"

"Sounds good." It would be good to start working on our first case.

"Good, I'll give him a call when we get back to the office. He mentioned something about an insurance claim. Pretty straightforward. Just need to keep an eye on the claimant for a day or two and see if he's incapacitated like he says. We can work on it together if you like, just until you get the hang of it," he added hastily.

"Great."

We finished our coffee and walked the few steps to the office. Bill called Stan while I checked the answering machine. Nothing. I wasted time shuffling papers around my desk while I waited for Bill to get off the phone.

"It's all set," he said as he came into my office. "Stan says he'll take ten percent on any referrals. I'll head over to his office and pick up the file. While I'm out I'm going to call on a few people I know, put out some feelers. Let's meet tomorrow morning at nine to plan how we're going to handle the investigation, okay?

"Sure, that's fine."

Bill left, and I looked around wondering what to do. I decided to call on some of the local businesses in the area and give them a brochure on our services:

divorce work, location of missing persons, insurance claims, internal fraud and theft. We hadn't said we'd find missing pets, but if the price was right, why not? I spent a pleasant afternoon getting reacquainted with the neighborhood, going home around five to find Gabby already in the middle of dinner preparations.

"Did you pick up the potatoes like I asked?" she questioned as I walked into the kitchen.

"Darn, I forgot." Actually I didn't even remember her saying anything about potatoes. "I'll run out right now and get some."

"Never mind, we'll have pasta instead. I know—you were so busy that you didn't have time," she teased.

"Not exactly."

I recounted my afternoon activities and told her about Bill's friend, Stan, and the file we were going to start working on the next day.

We decided to go to a movie after supper, so we rushed around getting our meal on the table, then ate quickly and made it to the seven o'clock showing. Afterward we went for coffee, then walked home. I went to bed early.

Bill beat me to the office the next day, so the coffee was ready when I arrived at nine. I grabbed a cup and we held our first case conference.

"Here's the story, Sam. This guy, Glen Peters, was in an accident, got rear-ended, not his fault. His claim's for personal injury—whiplash. Says he can't carry on his normal activities. He's pushing for a hefty settlement, pretty standard stuff in the industry. We need to follow him around for a couple of days and see what he can do. Either he's straight or he's crooked—we'll soon find out. What do you think? Do you want us to work on this together or can you handle it? It's okay with me either way." He closed the file and sat back, taking a gulp of his coffee.

"I can handle it," I said with more confidence than I felt. "I've had experience tailing someone." I was thinking of someone else I'd followed to find out where he lived. He'd caught me. I won't bother to go into all the gory details. This time I'd be more careful. "Should I take pictures?"

"Yeah, take the camera and the camcorder, too. If Peters decides to play tennis or something, it would be a good idea to get it on video."

"Okay, give me his address."

Bill gave me the file and I took it into my office to look it over. Peters lived in Saanich, a suburb a few miles east of the city. After I'd read over the file, I walked home quickly to pick up the van, a beat-up Westfalia camper living out its final days in the mild Victoria climate, and grabbed a sandwich, a couple of apples, and a can of juice. Telling Gabby I'd see her later, I left for Saanich.

I found the address easily, parked a few doors away, and took out my newspaper, pretending to read while I waited for something to happen. The house was a standard split-level, about thirty years old and well-kept, with a rental car in the driveway. The Peterses' car must still have been at the body shop for repairs after the accident.

A woman came out of the house just before noon

and drove off alone. Mrs. Peters? Where was Glen? I didn't have long to wait. Within a few minutes of her leaving, a guy came out of the house, went into the garage, and came out again with a bamboo rake. He had on a neck brace. He started cleaning the yard, raking leaves and debris from the flowerbeds in front of the house.

At first he moved slowly, as though in pain, but by the time he'd been at it for a while, he'd removed the brace, rolled up his sleeves, and was really going to town. He'd been working for about an hour when the woman came back, pulling into the driveway and going around to the passenger side of the vehicle to let out a small child. Probably their son.

The boy ran over to Peters, who picked him up and swung him high in the air over his head before depositing him on his shoulders. Then he galloped around the yard like a horse with a burr under its saddle. With the telephoto lens on the camera I got a few good shots of Peters playing horsey, then waited to see what he'd do next. The three of them went inside. I ate my lunch, wondering if I dared sneak away long enough to grab a coffee. Before I could make up my mind, Peters came out again, neck brace in place once more, and got into the car. He backed out of the driveway and started up the street.

I quickly started the van which, of course, was facing the wrong way, turned at the first corner, and headed back down the next street. I was hoping to catch him at the intersection. I caught a glimpse of his taillights as he turned again and headed toward the Pat Bay Highway and into town.

I managed to stay two or three vehicles behind Peters most of the way, then saw him turning left on Fort Street. He pulled up in front of an insurance office. He got the only unoccupied parking spot. Fort Street is one way going east. I circled the block, getting stuck behind a delivery truck, and stopped at a red light. By the time I arrived back at the insurance building, the rental vehicle was nowhere to be seen. I'd lost him.

It was only two o'clock so I decided to drive back to Saanich to see if he'd gone home. He hadn't. I waited the rest of the afternoon but he didn't show up. At five-thirty, I packed it in and headed back to the office, first dropping the used film at a one-hour developing outlet. I left a note for Bill, explaining what had happened and telling him I'd head back out to the Peters house first thing in the morning, then went home.

Mimi was mad at me. I'd left her home in the morning when I realized I'd be out all day, and she wasn't quick to forgive. I won her over with dog biscuits and by scratching her ears for what seemed like an interminable length of time.

Gabby wanted to hear about my day, so keeping my promise, I told her everything, even how I'd goofed up.

"Don't worry, you'll get the hang of it," she consoled. "You're a natural-born snoop."

Not knowing whether to take that as an insult or compliment, I decided to be pleased. Later, after enjoying a quiet dinner and classic movie on television, I said good night and went up to my room.

By nine the next morning, I was parked in front of

the Peters house, armed with a thermos of coffee and a huge sack of sandwiches, cookies, and fruit. It was a quiet morning. I read the newspaper back to front as is my habit and made a few notes for the next chapter of my book, working out a sticky problem between the two main characters.

By noon I'd drunk all the coffee. It was twelve-thirty when Peters finally came out of the house and set off down the street in the same direction as he'd gone the previous day. This time I'd parked on the opposite side of the street, so I could follow without having to turn around. Leaving a respectable distance between his vehicle and mine, I tailed him to the highway again. He headed toward town, then turned west on Hillside. Several turns later he ended up in a commercial area in front of a run-down warehouse.

There was nowhere for me to park and not be seen, so once he left his car and went into the warehouse, I drove past his vehicle and turned the corner. Taking a chance, I detoured to find a restroom at a nearby gas station. Professionals like James Bond and Superman never have to go hunting for washroom facilities, but I wasn't in their league.

Parking a couple of blocks away and tucking the camera inside my jacket, I walked slowly back toward the warehouse and Peters's parked vehicle.

From my position across the street, I could see several men working in shirtsleeves despite a chill in the March air. They were loading boxes into a large truck, which had pulled up next to the loading ramp. Peters was among them and he didn't seem to be having any problem lifting the boxes and carrying them from the warehouse to the truck along with the other men. Crossing the street and hiding behind the corner of the building, I took several shots of Peters and the others. Not only was he working, he was doing a job many people wouldn't be able to handle even without an injury. The insurance company would be interested in that. I tucked the camera back inside my jacket and turned to leave.

"What the heck are you doing here?" a rough voice behind me demanded.

My heart did a couple of somersaults, and I cleared my throat, all the while trying to think of a plausible explanation for my presence in the run-down industrial area. It seemed that while I had been busy snooping on the men, the truck driver had wandered away from the others to smoke a cigarette. I hadn't noticed him come up behind me. Had he seen the camera, I wondered? I hope not!

"I think I'm lost," I stammered lamely. "I was looking for Apex Machinery. I thought this was the right street but I must have been mistaken." I tried to look like a confused and helpless female, which wasn't hard, considering my predicament.

"Hey, Glen, you know this broad?" Grabbing my arm, he hollered over to Peters who separated himself from the others and came over.

Peters looked me up and down. "Nope, never seen her before. What do you want?" He didn't look menacing, just annoyed that the work had been interrupted.

I got my courage back. "As I was telling this big ape, I was looking for Apex Machinery. Isn't it somewhere in this area?"

"Let go of her, Jim," Peters told the driver.

The ape dropped his hand and I rubbed the spot on my arm gingerly.

"There's no Apex Machinery around here. You'd better get going, and be careful, this is a rough neighborhood," Peters warned.

"Yeah, thanks."

I didn't need a second warning. Turning and walking quickly to the van, I would not allow myself to falter or start shaking until I was inside the vehicle with the doors locked and the engine running. Close call! Why the heck were they so jumpy, anyway?

When I calmed down I drove back to the office, picking up the first set of pictures and dropping off the second roll of film on my way. Bill was nowhere to be seen. I typed a report for the insurance company, detailing what I'd seen but omitting that Peters had seen me. That information would only be shared on a need-to-know basis. Then after slipping out and picking up the second set of photos, I attached them to the report and put the whole thing on Bill's desk with an invoice clipped to the front, listing time spent, expenses, etc. Danger pay was merited for what I'd been through.

Gabby was out when I arrived home, so I started preparing supper. Even I can handle scrambled eggs and toast. When she got home she seemed pleased I'd made the effort and didn't complain about my lack of imagination, merely suggesting I try adding chopped chives or onions to the eggs next time to enhance the flavor.

After supper the phone rang, and I grabbed it, hoping it was Bill calling to say he'd seen my report. It wasn't. It was our neighbor, Mrs. Stevens, the elderly lady whose yard backed onto ours. She's the neighborhood busybody, not a bad soul, just a little lonely since her husband died a few years ago. She invited us for tea. I hollered at Gabby, and she said sure, so I told Mrs. Stevens we'd be over in a jiffy.

Walking around the block instead of cutting through the backyard gave us a little exercise. Mrs. Stevens was watching from her front room window and opened the door before we knocked.

"Gabby, how are you, dear?" She hugged Gabby, then patted my arm, knowing from past experience it wasn't worth the effort to try to hug me since I wasn't the touchy-feely type. "Sam, thanks for coming over. I especially wanted to ask your advice tonight. I have a little problem."

Uh-oh, what had she been up to? My first thought was that perhaps someone was suing her for invasion of privacy and she wanted me to recommend a good lawyer.

"Come on into the kitchen." She led us through the living room to the kitchen table where she'd set out three delicate blue-and-white china teacups with matching plates and tiny dessert forks. A big, fluffy chocolate cake sat in the middle of the table with a serving knife beside it.

"Sit down, sit down. I'll get the tea." She brought the kettle, which was simmering on the stove, back to a boil, rinsed out the teapot, and filled it up, tossing in two tea bags. Then she slipped a crocheted tea cozy over it and carried it to the table.

"Help yourselves to some cake. Sam, why don't you cut us each a slice? And be generous. I know how you like your sweets." She fussed around the table like a mother hen, pouring the tea and offering milk and sugar.

Cutting three hefty wedges of cake, I placed one on each plate, cleaned the icing off the knife with my finger, and licked my finger clean.

"Sam, where are your manners?" Gabby scolded, giving Mrs. Stevens one of those looks that cast aspersions on my upbringing and indicated she was trying her best to perform the impossible task of setting me straight. We both knew she was fighting a losing battle. "Don't mind her, Mrs. Stevens."

"Gabby, don't you think it's time you and Sam called me Mabel? We've known each other five years now."

"If you say so, Mabel."

The name was old-fashioned, but considering her age, appropriate. She was in her late seventies, small and quick with blue-rinsed gray hair and bright blue eyes that sparkled behind wire-framed glasses which, when they weren't perched on her nose, dangled from a gold chain around her neck. She'd gained a reputation, well-deserved, as the local gossip, but was also kind-hearted and generous, so people indulged her chatter without taking offense.

"Ready for more tea, Sam? And what about another piece of cake?" she coaxed.

"I couldn't." I groaned, wiping a few stray crumbs

off my face with the back of my hand. "I'm full. Just a little tea then, half a cup." I pushed the cup toward her and she filled it again.

"How's the new business going, Sam? Are you finding lots of clients?"

How the heck had she found out about us already? "We're just getting under way but we hope to build the business into something viable."

"I have a small favor to ask."

Uh-oh, why hadn't I seen this coming? "Oh, what's that?" I asked casually, cursing myself for being slow to pick up on her motive for the invitation.

"You know my sister, Ethel?"

I nodded. I'd never met Ethel but had heard Mabel talk about her as she did about everyone.

"Well, her granddaughter, Allison, has always been a wild girl, getting into trouble at school and running away from home. They've had a terrible time with her. I was talking to Ethel and mentioned your new business. I suggested she call you about Allison."

"I don't know if I can help," I said doubtfully. I wasn't a youth counselor. How could I help with a rebellious teenager?

"Oh, silly me," she tittered. "I forgot to mention the most important piece of information. Allison has disappeared—she's been gone a week. Ethel's very worried about her. She wants to talk to you about trying to find Allison and bringing her back home."

"Maybe she's just run away again and doesn't want to be found." I searched around for a good excuse not to get involved.

"Perhaps, but Ethel says she's never been gone

more than a couple of days before. She thinks something's happened to her. Would you mind talking to Ethel, perhaps making a few inquiries on her behalf? Allison's not a bad girl, just a little difficult."

"What do her parents have to say about her disappearance?"

"They think she's run away and will come back home when she runs out of money," Mabel said, shaking her head disapprovingly.

"Have they called the police to report her missing?"

"No, to tell you the truth, I think they find the whole situation a little embarrassing. Ethel's pleaded with them, but they say she shouldn't get involved."

"Well, perhaps she shouldn't," I countered.

"Allison is Ethel's granddaughter, after all." Mabel bristled. "And she and the girl have always been close. Ethel doesn't think Allison would go very far without letting her know her whereabouts. She's always stayed in touch before. Please, Sam, if you wouldn't mind talking to Ethel, I'd appreciate it. She's really worried."

"Okay," I gave in gracefully. Fishing in my pocket, I handed her one of my new business cards. "Ask her to call me tomorrow."

"Thank you, dear." Her relief was evident. "I'll call her tonight. Now have another piece of cake."

This time I accepted, feeling I deserved it. I would earn it when Ethel came to see me the next day. When I finished it off, picking up every last crumb from my plate with the end of my finger, Gabby and I said good-bye and walked home.

"Do you think you can help Mrs. Stevens's sister?"

Gabby asked. "I wonder what could have happened to her granddaughter."

"I don't know. I'll probably suggest she have the girl's parents call the police and report her missing. Bill might have some suggestions on how it should be handled. I don't mind making a few inquiries. After all, the phone's not exactly ringing off the hook." It wouldn't do any harm to make a few calls to help Mrs. Stevens's sister out and put her mind at ease. The girl probably wasn't far away, perhaps hiding from her parents at a friend's or hanging out at the malls. She'd turn up.

"Maybe my Psychic Circle could help," Gabby said thoughtfully.

"What could they possibly do?" I scoffed out loud before I could stop myself.

Gabby bristled. "Sam, don't laugh at the Circle—it's downright rude. Even some police departments use psychics to help locate missing persons. I'm going to mention Allison to the group and see if anyone can come up with anything in our next meditation."

Gabby's Psychic Circle met in our living room every Thursday night without fail to meditate and commune with the spirits.

"Okay, why not?" I backtracked quickly, thinking all the while they wouldn't learn a thing. It couldn't do any harm. What Gabby did was her business as long as she didn't drag me into it. I tried to be out of the house on Thursdays or, at the very least, made myself invisible, hiding upstairs in my room. "Yes," I repeated, "why not?"

Chapter Three

I hardly had my coat off and the coffee started the next morning, when the phone rang insistently.

"Hope and Henry, Sam speaking."

"Hello Sam, this is Ethel."

"Ethel?"

"Ethel Beauchamp, Mabel's sister."

"Mabel?"

"Mabel Stevens, your neighbor."

I still wasn't used to calling Mrs. Stevens Mabel and mornings are not my preferred time of day, so it took a minute to figure out just who Ethel was.

"Oh, Ethel, I'm sorry. I'm a little slow, haven't had my morning coffee yet," I offered by way of explanation. "How are you?"

"Fine thank you, Sam, but awfully worried about my granddaughter, Allison. She still hasn't come home. Mabel told you about her, I believe?"

"Yes, she mentioned you thought Allison had run away. How long has she been gone?"

"It's been a little more than a week. She's never been gone this long before."

"So she's been missing before?"

"Well, yes," she admitted reluctantly, "but never more than a day or two at the most. And she always calls to tell me where she is."

"And you haven't heard from her this time?"

"No, not since about five days ago. She called a couple of days after she left and told me not to worry. I haven't heard a thing since."

"So she did run away," I concluded.

"Yes, but from what she said on the phone, I got the impression she intended to stay away for a day or two, then go back home when her parents started to worry. Something must have happened to her."

"Have her parents called the police?"

"No, and I'm quite upset with them. They refuse to believe anything's wrong. They think she's just being difficult."

"Perhaps they have a point, Ethel," I said gently. "Maybe her parents are the best judge of what should be done."

"No," she insisted. "There's something wrong. Allison isn't a bad girl, just a little rebellious. She's been having problems with her parents, but she and I have always been close. She wouldn't let me worry needlessly. Something's definitely wrong."

"You'd better come into the office and we'll see what can be done. Can you make it in today? What about ten-thirty?"

"That would be fine. I'll see you then." I gave her the address and hung up.

Bill had come through the door while I was on the phone, and when I hung up he came out of his office.

"What's up?"

"You know Mrs. Stevens?" He nodded. He'd met her on several occasions. "Her sister's granddaughter has run away. She, I mean Mabel's sister, is coming to see me this morning. Do you want to sit in on the interview? She may or may not be a paying customer," I explained. "This may be just a favor for Mrs. Stevens."

"No thanks! I'm sure you can handle it. Stan sent another file over, so I'm going to be busy working on it for the next couple of days. By the way, thanks for the report on Peters. Any problems?"

"There *was* one small glitch, but I don't have time to explain now. Remind me later. I'm going out to pick up something to eat. I didn't bother with breakfast this morning. Do you want anything?"

"No, I'm off. I'll see you tomorrow then. If you need me, call me on the cell phone."

"Sure, talk to you later." I had barely enough time to dash out, pick up a Danish, and get back upstairs before Ethel arrived, knocking timidly on the outside door.

"Come on in, it's open," I called.

She poked her head around the corner, then advanced slowly into the room. "Sam? Ethel Beauchamp. We've never met, but I feel as though I know you. Mabel's told me all about you and Gabby."

I'll bet she has, I thought, but smiled and shook her

outstretched hand. Even if she hadn't introduced herself I would have known right away who she was. Another of the blue-rinse set, she bore a striking resemblance to her sister; the same bright blue eyes sparkled behind horn-rimmed glasses.

"How do you do, Ethel? You don't mind if I call you Ethel, do you? Come in and sit down." I led her over to the sofa and took a seat on the chair facing her.

"First of all, Sam, let me say how much I appreciate you seeing me. Mabel's told me how good you are at solving mysteries. This is terribly important. You'll be paid for your time. If you'll just tell me how much to make the check for, I'll give you one right now." She had pulled her check book out of her voluminous purse while she was talking and her pen was poised expectantly above it.

Although the situation felt a little awkward, I nevertheless explained we were paid by the hour for our services. Since I didn't know how much time it would take to find her granddaughter, I didn't know what she owed. I suggested she give me a retainer, naming a figure. She didn't even flinch as she wrote the check and signed it, handing it to me.

"Let's go into my office. I want to make notes while we talk and it'll be easier at my desk. Can I get you some tea or coffee before we start?"

"No, thanks."

"Okay, let's get busy. I should have asked you on the phone to bring a picture of Allison along. You wouldn't happen to have one in your bag, by any chance?"

"Yes, of course, what grandmother doesn't have photos of her grandchildren?" She smiled, reaching into her purse to pull out a small album. She flipped through the pages until she came to the one she was looking for, taking it out of its protective plastic cover and handing it to me.

I examined it closely. "She's very pretty."

"Yes, isn't she? You can't tell from that black-and-white photo, but she has striking auburn hair and green eyes. I can get you a more recent school picture. That one's a couple of years old."

"How old is Allison?"

"She's sixteen. Her birthday is June fifteenth, and she was born in 1980."

"So, she would be in about grade ten?"

"Yes, that's right. She's a good student, too, or at least she was until this past year or so when she started acting out, skipping classes, not doing her homework. Her parents have been back and forth to the school a lot lately."

"Is Allison your son's or daughter's child?"

"My daughter Judy's. Her last name is Gillespie."

"Did you tell your daughter and son-in-law you were coming to see me?"

"No, not yet." She looked sheepish. "I plan to talk to them this evening. I expect they'll be upset with me." She sighed, as if resigned to their disapproval.

"You know, I'll need to talk to Allison's parents to find out who her friends are, when she was last seen, what she was wearing, that sort of thing."

"Yes, I understand. I only hope they'll be willing to cooperate. My son-in-law, Darren, is very stubborn.

I'll try to convince him to let you make inquiries. I'm so worried." A tear rolled down her cheek and she pulled a lace-edged handkerchief out of her purse and dabbed at it.

"Don't worry, Ethel. I'll do my best to find her. If your son-in-law is willing to help it will be easier, but if he isn't, we'll find another way to get the information we need. Have *you* met any of Allison's friends?"

"There *is* one girl I've met several times. Her name is Melissa Egglington."

"By the way, you haven't mentioned where Allison lives."

"How silly of me." She gave a nervous giggle. "They're in Saanich on Poplar Street, and Allison's friend Melissa lives just around the corner on Larch. If you give me a piece of paper, I'll write down the address and phone number." She pulled a small address book out of her seemingly bottomless bag and looked up the information. Writing it down, she handed it to me. "There you are. And now I'd better go." She stood up. "Please wait until I call you later today or tomorrow before contacting my daughter. I'll talk to her and her husband and get back to you as soon as possible."

"That's fine. I'll wait until you call." I walked her to the door, closing it after her.

After lunch, I sat at my desk thinking about Allison Gillespie and studying her photo. Her face was pretty but she had a sullen, spoiled look as if bored by life. Imagine being bored at sixteen. What would her life be like in twenty years? She had long wavy hair and wore a lot of makeup, especially dark eyeliner and mascara. She looked a lot like a little girl who'd gotten into her mother's cosmetics on the sly.

I made up a file and entered all the information I had so far into the computer, printing off a copy to take home. It was Thursday, so I expected to go into hiding in my room while the Psychic Circle met downstairs. I would give Allison's picture to Gabby to show to the Circle and see what they came up with. I didn't expect much—in fact, nothing.

Gabby had supper ready, a delicious vegetable casserole with a creamy cheese sauce, which she served over pasta. As we ate, I told her about my conversation with Ethel Beauchamp and showed her Allison's picture. She agreed to show it to the Circle and let me know what they had to say. After supper she went to change while I washed and dried the dishes and put on a pot of coffee, setting out mugs and a plate of cookies for the group. When the doorbell rang, I grabbed a mug of coffee and a couple of cookies and beat it upstairs, taking Clem and Mimi with me.

It would be hours before everyone went home so I passed the time by making a list of tasks for myself. As soon as Ethel called I would get started. It couldn't take more than a few days to track down a runaway in Victoria. As cities go, it's on the small side and situated on an island—a closed environment. If Allison hadn't left the lower island, she should be easy to find. I made a note to myself to ask Ethel if Allison had any money. When I was finished, I curled up on the couch with a book and must have dozed off. The next thing I remember was being shaken awake by Gabby.

"Sam, wake up."

"What? What's wrong?" I sat up quickly and looked around.

"You fell asleep. It's ten o'clock."

"Ten?" I was groggy and disoriented, not sure if she meant morning or night.

"Everyone's gone home. The Circle, silly. We had our meditation. You've got to hear what happened," she added excitedly, plopping down next to me on the couch.

I rubbed my eyes, feeling drugged. Too many late nights, getting the business off the ground. "What's up?"

"Everyone in the group agreed the girl didn't run away. I mean she ran but had no intention of staying away. Something terrible has happened to her. Everyone agreed on that. But the group was divided on exactly what."

Gabby repeated all of this as if it were gospel and must be believed. I tried to hide my skepticism.

"Betty and Sandi said they saw a body in a wooded area near water. Stephanie saw danger but not death. You'd better find her quickly." She handed me the picture, her eyes wide and worried.

"This is ridiculous!" I said, perhaps a trifle too quickly. But if she was trying to make me worried about the girl, she was succeeding. "She's just gone AWOL on her parents. She's probably hiding out at a friend's. As far as I can tell no one has checked."

"Sam, it's more serious than that," Gabby explained

patiently, as if speaking to a small child. "Listen to me, the girl's in trouble."

"Well, thank the Circle for me, Gabby. I appreciate the info," I said, trying to stifle a yawn.

"No you don't. Sometimes you can be so annoying, Sam." Losing her cool, she jumped up and marched out of the room leaving me sitting there scratching my head. Normally she had a placid, unflappable disposition, but when she lost her temper it was like an explosion. No use apologizing until the dust had settled.

I put the dogs outside for a run, turned out lights around the house, and then letting them back in, went upstairs. Gabby's door was shut so I hugged the dogs and went, chastened, to bed.

There was no call from Ethel the next morning, only a couple of inquiries from people asking about our rates. One was from a woman who intimated she might want to have her husband followed. She seemed convinced he was seeing someone and wanted to get enough evidence for a divorce. I took the details and left a message for Bill to call her when he came in. It sounded like the sort of investigation that would be more up his alley than mine.

While waiting for Ethel's call, I phoned all the hospitals in and around Victoria, checking to see if there'd been anyone admitted who fit Allison's description. There was no one and no young Jane Does at the morgue either. That was good news.

By lunchtime, I still hadn't heard from Ethel, so I went home. On the way, Mimi and I walked through

James Bay's commercial area, stopping at the local Credit Union to deposit Ethel's check in our business account. Mimi watched from outside as I chatted with the teller. On my way out the door, I bumped into our neighbor, Jill Stone, who lived in the apartment adjoining ours. She and George, who'd recently been married, had just come back from a delayed honeymoon in Mexico. She'd had her hair cut short, lost a few pounds, and looked great.

"Sam, it's so good to see you."

Before I could avoid it she gave me a hug, and then laughed when I squirmed uncomfortably.

"You, too. You look tanned and happy." Her freckles, which seemed to have multiplied in the Mexican sun, stood out in sharp relief on her pretty face.

"We had a great time. Are you going home for lunch?"

"Yup, what about you?"

"Yes, hold on a minute, I want to withdraw some money, then I'll walk back with you."

Mimi and I waited outside the Credit Union while Jill worked her way through the line, then joined us. We started up the sidewalk, turning the corner onto St. Vincent Street.

"Wasn't that terrible news about the young girl found out at Elk Lake this morning?"

My heart stood still. "I haven't heard the news today. What do you mean? Did they say who she was?"

"You mean you haven't heard? A body was discovered at the lake. She's been identified—and Elisabeth knew her," she added importantly. Elisabeth is Jill's older daughter. "She played volleyball against her in the high school league. The girl was only sixteen. Such a pity. I think her name was Alicia—no, that's not right. Allison? Yes, Allison, that's it. I don't remember the last name, but Elisabeth would know it. She was quite upset. She heard it on the news just before leaving for school."

"Oh dear, so that's why I haven't heard from Ethel this morning." I picked up the pace, anxious to get home and call Mabel for more details.

"Who's Ethel?"

"Mrs. Stevens's sister. She came to see me yesterday about her granddaughter, Allison Gillespie, who's been missing for the past week. It sounds very much as though it may have been Allison's body that was found at the lake. This is terrible. Ethel will be so upset."

"Oh, that's so sad." We went through the gate and up the front stairs of the house.

"Jill, I may want to talk to Elisabeth later if that's all right with you to ask her a few questions about Allison."

"No problem, Sam, I'm sure she'll want to help if she can. We'll talk later." She opened her door and went inside.

I unlocked our door and stepped into the hallway with Mimi, stopping to greet Clem as usual. The dogs remained unruffled by the tragedy. All they knew was that their owners were both home at last.

Gabby called to me from the kitchen. "Sam, in here."

I walked slowly through the house, removing my coat and tossing it on the love seat in the living room.

"Have you heard the news?" she asked soberly.

"I just met Jill and we walked home from the Credit Union together. She told me Allison's body has been found. What have you heard?"

"A news report, a few minutes ago, on the radio. They have positively identified a body found at Elk Lake as Allison Gillespie. She's been dead for a couple of days. They don't know the cause of death yet. Mabel will be so upset and so will her sister." Gabby paused. "Sam, isn't this just what some of the Circle saw in our meditation last night? Betty and Sandi both said they saw a body in a wooded area. And Betty said it would be found near water. Allison's body was found in Elk Lake, in a small bay surrounded by a wooded area. So they were right." She paused, then continued. "But don't feel too badly, Sam. It looks as though she may have died before you even talked to Ethel Beauchamp. There was nothing you could have done."

"No." I hesitated. "Maybe not, but perhaps there's something I can do now."

"What do you mean? I'm sure the police will investigate and find out what happened to her, Sam. Leave it to them." She continued setting the table for lunch.

"I've got to get a hold of Ethel. She gave me a check. I wonder if she wants it returned, or if Bill and I should try to find out what happened to Allison. Give me a few minutes and I'll be back down for lunch." I ran upstairs to the office where Gabby operates her business—where my desk and the phone are located—and quickly dialed Mabel's number.

"Mabel, it's Sam," I said when she picked up the phone.

"Sam, I'm so glad you've called. Ethel's here with me. Isn't it dreadful? I can't believe it's Allison they found but the police say she's been positively identified. We're both in shock. Ethel would like to talk to you. Can you possibly come over?"

"How about in an hour, around two o'clock? Would that be okay?"

"That's fine. Thank you, dear." She hung up.

I went slowly back downstairs to Gabby. "I talked to Mabel. I'm going to go and see her and Ethel at two. Ethel's at her place right now."

"Seriously, Sam, shouldn't you leave the investigation of Allison's death to the police? You don't know if foul play's involved or if her death was accidental. Nothing is known at this point. Don't you think the police are better equipped to investigate her death?"

"I'll see what Ethel thinks, maybe that's how she'll feel, too. Let's have lunch and we'll talk later, after I've been over to see them."

We ate in silence. I did the dishes while Gabby went upstairs to work. When the kitchen was tidy, I went through the back gate to Mabel's, climbing the steps to knock on the door. The two sisters were visible through the kitchen window, seated at the table with cups of tea in front of them. Mabel got up to open the door when she heard me.

"Come in, Sam." She turned automatically to the cupboard to take down another cup and saucer and silently poured some tea, motioning to the chair beside Ethel.

"Ethel, I'm so sorry to hear about Allison. This must be a real shock to you and her parents."

"Thank you, Sam. I can hardly believe it, yet in a way I've been steeling myself against this news for a few days. I knew she would have called if she could." She reached up with her handkerchief to dab at her eyes.

"Do the police know what happened to her?"

"Details are still sketchy. All they've told us is that a jogger was out last evening and stumbled across her body beside the trail alongside Elk Lake. I had persuaded my son-in-law to call the police yesterday after I spoke to you. When the body was discovered, the police suspected it might be Allison so they called Darren to the hospital to identify her. I guess there was some decomposition as she'd been out in the elements for a few days."

This revelation was too much for her. She dissolved in tears and Mabel rushed to comfort her, wiping away her own tears.

"Have they any idea how she died?"

"Not yet. They're talking about suicide, but I can't accept that. Allison was mixed-up and rebellious, but not suicidal."

"When will they have the results of the autopsy?"

"I don't think we'll hear anything before Monday. They told us the body will be released for burial as soon as the results are known. That means Monday or Tuesday. Her parents are planning a funeral for next Thursday."

"Ethel, I deposited your check into our account at the Credit Union before I heard the news. I'll write you one this afternoon and deliver it later if you like."

She turned quickly. "No, don't do that. Hang on to the money for now, Sam. I may want you to look into Allison's death. If the police decide she committed suicide, I won't accept it. Even if we had a little more information about the events leading to her death, I might be able to let her rest. If you don't mind waiting until next week, I'll be in touch."

"No problem. If there's anything I can do in the meantime, let me know." I finished my tea and got up to leave.

Mabel came to the door with me. "This is just terrible, Sam. Anything you can do to help the family would be appreciated. I'll be in touch. Thanks for coming over so quickly."

Instead of going home, I went straight to the office, hoping to catch Bill. He was on the phone. As I waited, I wondered what help we might be able to provide Allison's family. Even if the girl's death had been suicide the family might want to know what had happened the last few days of her troubled life. By talking to her friends and retracing her steps, I might be able to discover a reason for her untimely death.

"Hi Sam, what's up?" Bill asked as he hung up.

"Have you been listening to the news? That girl I was supposed to try to locate has turned up dead."

His eyebrows raised. "That's too bad. What happened?"

I told him what I knew, which wasn't much, and

asked what he thought we should do, explaining about the check.

"Why don't you see what develops over the next couple of days? When Ethel gets back to you, we can decide if there's a role for us—how does that sound?"

"Sounds good. She'll likely call after Monday when the results of the autopsy are known."

"Why don't you go home now? Take it easy, relax over the weekend. Emily and I are going to Vancouver this weekend to take in a show. We'll be back Sunday night, and I'll call you then. We can meet here Monday morning, let's say nine. I want to tell you about the case I'm working on, too."

"Agreed." I cleaned up my desk, shut down the computer, and walked home. Gabby had gone out, so the dogs and I went for a brisk walk through Beacon Hill Park to the ocean. As I walked through a densely wooded area in the park, thoughts about the gruesome discovery made in the woods around Elk Lake came to the surface of my mind. I shuddered and quickened my pace, breaking into a clearing. The dogs scampered ahead, oblivious to my somber thoughts. There was no point dwelling on what had happened. I would try to push those thoughts back down until after the weekend.

We arrived home muddy and exhausted about the time Gabby pulled up in front of the house. As we went inside I filled her in on my conversation with Ethel and Mabel, suggesting we shelve all discussion of Allison until we heard from Ethel on Monday. She agreed, relieved the investigation was on hold.

As I went through the weekend, carrying on with

my normal routine, shopping for groceries, walking the dogs, watching a movie that had just come out on video, my thoughts kept straying back to an unhappy sixteen-year-old lying still and cold in the woods.

Chapter Four

The weekend passed quickly and before I knew it, I was back in the office at nine A.M. Monday morning, clutching my first coffee of the day. Bill had not yet put in an appearance. As I contemplated calling him and dragging him out of bed, Mimi barked, and I heard footsteps on the stairs outside the office. He threw opcn thc door and bustled in carrying a bag of something that smelled delectable.

"Anybody here want a fresh, warm doughnut?" Mimi wagged her whole body in anticipation.

"Trade you one for a hot coffee," I said, getting up to pour him a cup.

"Have you been waiting long?" he asked.

"Just long enough to brew the coffee. How was your weekend?"

"Great, we had a ball." His voice was full of enthusiasm. "Emily's so much fun. We caught that show I was telling you about, hit a couple of great restaurants, even went dancing—she's certainly gotten me out of my rut." Bill smiled, sitting back on the couch and putting his feet on the coffee table.

"Amazing how a beautiful, intelligent woman will do that," I teased.

"So what did you get up to this weekend? You didn't spend the whole time stewing about the girl, did you?"

"I tried not to, but it was difficult. I didn't do much, the usual shopping, laundry—you know, *my* rut," I tried to joke.

"Grab another coffee and let's get to work."

I refilled my cup and sat back down.

"Stan has thrown a couple of more cases our way, same sort of thing as the Peters case. And we had a call from a woman who suspects her husband of cheating and wants him followed. Oh, I forgot, you took that call, didn't you?"

"Yeah, and don't forget, Ethel's money is still in our account at the Credit Union. I'm expecting to hear today whether she wants it back or wants us to look into her granddaughter's death."

"There could be a role for us, as long as we don't get in the way of the police. How about I call the detachment and see who's working on the file? We can find out if the autopsy results are in and let them know we may be working on it."

"Good idea. In the meantime, do you want me to take on one of the insurance files? I'll leave the errant husband to you."

"Sounds good." He handed me the file to take into my office.

This time the claimant's address was in Fairfield, just on the other side of Beacon Hill Park from James Bay. A woman in her thirties by the name of Jessie Calder was claiming serious back problems and an inability to look after her children as she had done before the accident. I checked the cameras for film, then set off to pick up the van. So far, sharing the van with Gabby had worked out fine as she worked at home most of the time. But if we got busier I might have to think about picking up a small car to run around in, something like Emily's little Volkswagen Golf would be nice, I thought. I'd borrowed it once and had enjoyed its easy handling and power compared to the van.

The van was parked in front of the house. I went inside to let Gabby know I was taking it, packed a lunch, and took off, once again leaving Mimi at home. She watched mournfully at the door as it closed behind me, locking hcr in. Dogs! They have a knack for making a person feel guilty.

I headed up the street, cut through the park, and came out on Cook Street. A couple of turns and I found the Calder house, a turn-of-the-century home with a beautiful stained-glass window above the door. The house had been painted several shades of green with small areas highlighted in deep maroon. It was charming and definitely more pricey than the Peters home. I was going up in the world, staking out a classier neighborhood. Parking on the opposite side of the street a couple of doors down from the Calders, I took out a book I'd been trying to get into for weeks, all the while keeping one eye on the house.

I must have sat for over two hours before there was any action at all. Finally a woman came out the front door and started down the stairs. She appeared to be in her late thirties but was bent over as though much older and using a cane. That must be Jessie.

She made her way slowly and painfully, if the expression on her face was any indication, to a vehicle parked in front of the house. Getting in carefully, she started the engine and drove off. I got myself turned around and caught up with her. When she got onto Cook Street, she parked in front of the Royal Bank and went inside, coming out a few moments later and walking slowly down the street toward Starbucks. As she went inside, I parked, then followed her into the espresso bar. She didn't know me; I could sit right next to her and enjoy a cappuccino and she'd have no idea she was being watched.

She met a woman who was already seated at one of the tables. The woman got up to give her a hug, settled her into a chair, and went to get her a coffee. I got in line behind the woman and ordered cappuccino with extra foam, then took a seat at an adjacent table, close enough to overhear their conversation.

"How are you feeling, Jessie?"

"Not very well," Jessie complained in a voice bordering on a whine. "It's so frustrating. My back seems to be taking forever to heal. There are so many things I can't do. I can't vacuum or wash floors, not that I miss that much." She smiled weakly. "But I can't even bathe the kids by myself. Ryan helps, but he's out of town a lot. I really need a housekeeper or someone to come in each day, but the insurance company doesn't want to pay and since I'm not working right now, I can't afford to hire one myself. Sometimes I wonder if they think I'm faking." She started to cry. "Why would I do that? I'd give anything to be able to bathe my own kids again."

Her friend patted her hand. "It's all right. What does the doctor say?"

"He says my back will get better but it takes time. He says be patient, rest the muscles as much as possible, and don't be pushed into doing things I can't handle. Easier said than done." She grimaced as she tried to shift in her chair.

I stirred my coffee guiltily, feeling mean and nasty to be spying for the bad, old insurance company. She was obviously in pain. It looked as though the company had made a mistake on this file. But just to make sure, I figured I should stay on the case for a day or two before sending in my report.

She got up to leave and after a short interval I went too, cruising past the house again. She had come straight home and was making her way up the stairs. She stayed in the rest of the day.

In the middle of the afternoon, a young boy and girl who looked to be about five and six came running down the sidewalk, lunchboxes swinging, and turned into the yard, going around the side of the house. Must have been the kids she had mentioned.

I watched a while longer, but when no one came out again and it started to get dark, I drove home. On my way through the park, I thought about what my workdays were like now compared to a few short weeks ago. I had a new lease on life. Each day was different—no more sitting at a desk for eight hours a day. Granted, there wasn't much money coming in yet, but I was confident it would. Yes, quitting my job to go into business with Bill had definitely been a good decision. The only snag was there never seemed to be time to work on my book. It was as bad as before. I'd have to come up with a schedule that allowed me to spend time on it each day or it would always take a back seat to other, seemingly more important, activities.

From home I called the answering machine at the office to pick up any messages. There was nothing urgent. Then I called Bill's cell phone to see if he'd taken a call from Ethel. He'd just arrived home and said he'd been out of the office all day and hadn't taken any calls. He hadn't had a call back from the detachment that was responsible for investigating Allison's death, either.

So Ethel hadn't phoned. I'd give her another day, then call her to see what had happened. She should know by then what the police had discovered, if anything.

Tuesday was a miserably cold, rainy day. Mimi, who hates the rain, stuck her head out the door and scurried back to her mat in the kitchen. She made it quite clear she had no intention of venturing out. I felt more or less the same and took my time getting ready for work. I didn't reach the office until after ten.

Bill was waiting for me. "How did you make out

with that file on the Calder woman?" he asked after I had hung up my wet things and poured myself a coffee.

"You mean Jessie? I followed her around all day. She doesn't look like she's faking to me. I was planning on checking on her a couple more times before writing my report, though, just to be sure."

"Well, not every person the insurance company thinks is defrauding them really is. Only a small percentage of claimants would think of doing such a thing and even less actually do."

"How did you make out?" I asked.

"Our client's husband is definitely out for a good time. He has not only one but two women on the side. His wife's money will be well spent. She'll get her divorce all right. It'll take a couple of days to wrap up the file, then I'll be looking around for something else to do."

"Did Ethel call this morning?"

"Not since I've been here. Why don't you call her?"

"I might just do that but first I promised myself two hours on the book today and I have a sneaking feeling I'd better put in the time first." Turning on the computer, I got to work.

The phone rang some time later and I picked it up absentmindedly.

"Hello, Hope and Henry."

"Sam, you coming home for lunch?"

"What time is it?" I glanced at my watch. "It's one already? The time just slipped away. Be right home."

I saved the document I was working on and quickly

threw on my jacket, grabbed my umbrella, and ran downstairs. Lunch was ready so we sat down right away. After our meal Gabby went upstairs to work and I drove to the Calder residence to set up my James Bond operation again.

At a little after two o'clock, a black, older-model Mercedes pulled up behind the van and parked. A man in his late thirties got out and went across the street. He walked around the side of the Calder house and disappeared. Just then I spotted another car coming down the street. It pulled alongside the van. It looked familiar, but I wasn't really paying attention to anything but what might be going on at the house, so I wasn't at all prepared to see Bill lean over and roll down the car window. What the heck was he up to?

"What are you doing here?" he asked, giving me a puzzled look. He obviously hadn't been expecting to see me, either.

"I should be asking you that. This is Jessie Calder's place."

"Well, I'll be . . ." He chuckled. "That guy who just went inside is the wandering husband of *my* client."

"Hmm, looks like our two investigations just became one. So, what do we do now? Do you want to stay and keep a lookout or should I?" I asked, marveling at the bizarre turn of events.

"I'll stay," Bill volunteered. "I wonder what the heck's going on."

"Looks like he's got a third woman on the string. And maybe Jessie's not in as much pain as I thought. I'd like to be a fly on the wall in there."

"You scoot on back to the office. I'm going to check this out." He reached over to roll the window back up.

"Yes, sir," I said, saluting facetiously, and started the engine. As I drove away, he pulled into my parking spot. I returned to the office by way of the usual shortcut through the park. Back at the office, the answering machine blinked insistently. Punching the button, I listened to the message.

"Sam, it's Ethel. We need to talk. Please call me as soon as you get in."

I grabbed her file to check the phone number and punched it in with one hand as I took off my jacket with the other.

"Hello?" Ethel's voice quavered.

"Ethel, it's me, Sam. How are you?"

"About as well as can be expected, Sam. It's a very difficult time for all of us."

"I'm sure it is. Have your daughter and son-in-law heard from the police?"

"Yes, that's what I'm calling about. I think I'd better come down to the office to see you. Would tomorrow morning be convenient?"

"Certainly, let's say ten o'clock?"

"I'll be there. Thanks, Sam. Good-bye."

"See you tomorrow." Darn, now I'd have to wait another day to find out what the police had discovered. I tidied the office and, feeling at loose ends, left a little early. One of the perks of being my own boss.

Ethel was right on time. As the Dominion Time Signal on CBC radio sounded ten o'clock, she knocked and walked into the office. She'd aged in the past few days. The plain black coat and hat she was wearing didn't help, making her look old, tired, and sad.

"Come in, Ethel." I put a hand under her elbow and lead her to the sofa. "Have a seat. Would you like a cup of coffee?"

"Yes, please. Black, no sugar." I poured a fresh cup for her and one for myself then sat down, waiting for her to begin.

"Well, Sam, it's as I feared. The police have decided Allison's death was either an accident or suicide. The autopsy showed she'd had a small amount of alcohol. They seem to feel she became despondent and went to the lake by herself, either deliberately or accidentally fell into the water and drowned. They say there was no sign of a struggle, and she had not been assaulted, thank heaven for that, so they don't feel anyone else was involved."

"What does her family have to say?"

"Not much; they're still in shock. My son-in-law seems pretty quick to accept the notion that Allison would have gone to the lake and accidentally thrown herself in. I'm not. I don't believe a word of it. I've never known Allison to drink. Furthermore, she was afraid of water. She didn't know how to swim and always avoided being around water. I can't believe, if she had decided to kill herself, she'd have chosen drowning. Suicide's out of the question," Ethel said firmly. "Despite being mixed-up and rebellious, Allison was not an unhappy girl. She no more wanted to kill herself than I do. There's something fishy about this, Sam. Will you keep that retainer and look into

Allison's death, please?" She sat back, waiting anxiously for my response.

I didn't hesitate. I wanted to try to find out what had happened. My own teenage years had been more than a little rebellious, especially after the shocking news of my father. I felt sympathy for the little girl that I'd seen in the picture.

"I'm willing to learn what I can about her death, Ethel, but I'd like to think your daughter and son-in-law approve, or at least agree with my involvement, before I start."

"Darren doesn't approve, but he *did* agree I had the right to spend my money however I liked. He said he and Judy would talk to you about Allison and give you whatever information you need."

"That's good enough for me. Let's get to work." I got out my notebook and went over the notes I'd made the last time Ethel had been in the office. She added everything else she could think of. When she left, I started getting organized.

Where to begin? It might be a good idea to attend Allison's funeral the next day to get a look at her parents and friends before calling on them. Ethel had told me the service would be held at Grayson's Funeral Chapel on Quadra Street at one o'clock.

As I sat there mapping out my action plan, Bill came up the stairs at a run. He threw open the door.

"Sam, I missed you yesterday afternoon. I got back just before five."

"I left a little early," I said guiltily, until I realized what I was doing. Bill was not my boss any more than I was his.

"You'll never believe what our two pigeons were up to after you left." He chortled gleefully. "I went around to the backyard and up onto the porch. I could see into the house. They were kissing and hugging—getting *very* close. I have to say, Sam, there's nothing wrong with Jessie's back." Bill looked as pleased as punch at himself for having caught Jessie red-handed.

I laughed out loud, visualizing Bill on the porch peering in the window like a Peeping Tom.

"And I've got pictures. Talk about killing two birds with one stone. My client's going to be pleased and so is the insurance company." Bill's face was smug and just a little superior.

"Well, she sure had me fooled," I grumbled. It annoyed the heck out of me that Bill had been the one to get the goods on her.

"You and a lot of other people, including her husband, I'll bet."

"I can't believe you went up on the porch and looked in the window. What if they'd seen you?" Obviously I had a lot to learn about the P.I. business.

"Then I'd make like I was the gas man reading the meter or someone looking for odd jobs. Don't worry, I can look after myself. But don't you go trying a stunt like that," he warned in that annoyingly patronizing tone he likes to use.

"Why not? If you can do it, why can't I?" I challenged, my chin going up and fists clenching as though ready to do battle.

"Because it could be dangerous," Bill explained patiently, speaking as if to a small child.

"Bill, don't start with that chauvinistic garbage," I

issued my own warning, my face turning red. "You know I take it as a personal challenge. You make me want to do something crazy, just to prove I can."

"Okay, okay," he conceded quickly. "Just be careful. Now what have you been up to?"

"Ethel was here. You just missed her. The police told the family they think Allison's death was an accident or possibly suicide. Ethel doesn't agree and wants me to look into it. I thought I'd start by talking to the girl's family and friends. See if I can find out what she did the last few days before her death—who saw her last, how she was feeling, that sort of thing."

"Sounds like a plan. But like I said, be careful and call on me for help if you need it."

"Don't worry, I will," I said, brushing aside his offer. I was going to handle this investigation myself just to prove I could. "By the way, did you manage to get a hold of anyone at the detachment?"

"No, they never called back."

"Well, never mind for now. Let me see what I can find out."

I didn't want to start interviewing Allison's friends until after the funeral, so at lunch, I decided to play hooky and go for a drive somewhere where I could give the dogs a good run. I thought of French Beach Provincial Park, an hour's drive away. The weather had broken and although it was cold, the sun was shining. If I bundled up it would be pleasant.

Chapter Five

The day of Allison's funeral was dark and cold, with a storm brewing, as though the gods were in mourning for the young woman. Not expecting to get much work done, I went to the office anyway and plugged away at the computer, keeping my promise to myself to put in a couple of hours on the book each morning. Bill wasn't in, so Mimi kept me company, and I worked quietly until after eleven, then went home to change and have lunch before attending the service.

Gabby was upstairs in her room, in the process of changing into a black dress and hunting in the bottom of her closet for matching shoes. Seeing her dressed in black brought home the reality of the situation—the dress was a far cry from her trademark bright colors and patterns.

"Sam, you'd better change quickly while I run

downstairs and make us a sandwich. We don't want to be late for the service."

"I'm glad you're coming along. I need the moral support." I've never been much good at funerals, but then who is?

We ate quickly, grabbed coats and umbrellas, and hurried out to the van. By the time we'd driven the short distance to the funeral home, my black pantsuit and Gabby's dress were completely covered in curly white dog hairs—the downside to owning sheepdogs. I hauled out the clothes brush we always carried in the glove compartment for just such emergencies. We brushed ourselves off and quickly joined the other people filing into Grayson's Funeral Home.

The chapel was crowded, but we managed to find two seats near the back of the room, which suited me fine. We were perfectly situated to watch the other mourners without being observed. Not only was I there to pay my respects to Allison's family, I was also on duty.

The room had been decorated with spring flowers, tulips and daffodils, appearing almost festive in spite of the solemn occasion. A closed casket, covered by a blanket of white roses, was situated at the front of the chapel.

It appeared as though all of Allison's classmates had turned out for the funeral. There were several rows of somber, uncomfortable kids dressed in dark colors, with the usual array of green and orange hair, nose rings, and black leather. Some were whispering to one another but most seemed awed by their surroundings and sat quietly. Some of the girls were crying. It was unusual to see so many teenagers at a funeral and it didn't seem right somehow that these young kids should have to face the reality of death. I wondered which of the young women was Melissa Egglington, Allison's best friend.

Glancing around the room, I tried to spot Mabel Stevens and her sister Ethel. They didn't seem to have arrived. Then I noticed a curtained room to one side of the chapel which was, apparently, a private room just for family members. Through the opaque drapery, I could make out several people I didn't know and among them sat the two elderly ladies.

The service began promptly at one o'clock. A minister spoke briefly about Allison, in words general enough to make it obvious he hadn't known her personally. A woman sang "Amazing Grace" and "The Lord is My Shepherd," and prayers were repeated. Then a young woman got up and walked to the front of the room. She introduced herself as Melissa Egglington and talked about her friendship with Allison, referring to notes on a crumpled piece of paper. She said she and Allison had started school together, gone to each other's birthday parties, played volleyball and basketball together, and double-dated. Hankies were evident throughout the audience, as people identified with the close bond between the girls, realizing how difficult it would be for Melissa in the days to come.

Toward the end of her speech, Melissa was overcome with emotion, unable to finish. One of the other girls came up to the front and helped her back to her seat. The minister led a final prayer and at the end of the service announced that coffee and tea would be served in a small reception room to the right of the chapel. The organist continued to play as people filed out of the room. Some folks went outside to smoke or talk quietly, while others went straight to the reception area to visit with family members whom they hadn't had a chance to speak to due to the arrangement of the rooms.

While Gabby waited in the reception room, I ducked outside. I'd noticed Melissa with her girlfriend and a young man making their way through the front door. I hoped to corner her before she disappeared. Most of the young people seemed to be headed outside.

There was a school bus parked outside. The kids must have come straight from school. Some of them had climbed back onto the bus, others stood talking and hugging one another.

I made my way quickly to the small group where Melissa was standing. "Melissa?"

She looked up, her eyes red-rimmed and swollen. "Who are you?" She regarded me sullenly and I was reminded of the picture of Allison. Her eyes were ringed with black where her mascara had run, giving her raccoon eyes.

"Samantha Hope. I'm a friend of Allison's grandmother. She told me you were Allison's closest friend." This statement brought a fresh round of tears and the offer of a tissue from the girl standing beside her.

"That's right," she said defiantly, as if I'd accused her of being an ax murderer.

"Allison's grandmother has asked me to look into her death. Can we talk?" She started to protest so I added quickly, "I don't mean right now. Perhaps we could meet tomorrow after school. I'll buy you a Coke or something?"

There was a hasty conference with her friends, then she responded, "I guess so."

"How about I pick you up in front of the school?"

"Okay, I'll be ready at three-thirty."

"That's fine. What school do you go to?"

There was a chorus of replies. "West Saanich Secondary."

"It's on West Saanich Road," Melissa added.

"Okay, I'll see you in front of the school tomorrow at three-thirty." The bus driver honked and the kids made their way toward the bus. As soon as the last one climbed in, the driver closed the door and pulled out of the parking lot.

Inside the chapel I made my way into the reception. As I scanned the room trying to locate Gabby, I spotted a familiar face in the crowd. What the heck was Glen Peters doing at Allison's funeral? The last time I'd seen him he was hefting boxes at that run-down warehouse. He and a woman who looked like his wife were standing to one side, drinking coffee and talking to each other. He was wearing his neck brace. They didn't appear to know anyone.

I spotted Gabby talking to Mabel and went over to them.

"There you are, Sam. I was just telling Mabel I'd lost track of you. There are so many people here," Gabby said, looking around.

"I was outside talking to some of Allison's friends. Mabel, do you see that man and woman standing by themselves?" I gestured in the direction of Peters and his wife. "Do you know who they are?"

"No, I've never seen them before. Perhaps they're friends of Darren and Judy's."

"By the way, can you point out Ethel's daughter and son-in-law to me? I haven't met them yet."

She looked around the room. "There they are, over by the exit." She pointed to a tall man with sandy hair and a mustache and an attractive, red-haired woman beside him. I was struck by the fact that I'd seen more grief outside on the faces of Allison's friends than I could see on theirs, especially her father's. Perhaps they were in shock.

"I'd like to go and offer my condolences. Excuse me a moment."

I walked swiftly over to where they stood saying good-bye to another couple. They turned to greet me, realized they hadn't a clue who I was, and stood awkwardly waiting for me to speak.

"Mr. and Mrs. Gillespie? I'm Samantha Hope, a friend of Mabel's. Please accept my condolences on the loss of your daughter."

"Ms. Hope." Darren Gillespie shook my hand. "This is my wife, Judy." I held out my hand and she put hers weakly into it, then drew it away quickly as though afraid of catching a communicable disease. She appeared to be drugged. I supposed it was her way of getting through the ordeal.

"Darren, I see you've met Sam." Ethel, who'd seen us talking, approached from a short distance away.

"Oh, is this the Sam whom you've asked to look into Allison's death?" He turned to me again, his expression more wary and less polite than a moment before. "Ms. Hope, my mother-in-law and I are not in agreement on the necessity of engaging you to investigate Allison's death. What possible good can come of it? It's much too late to be of any help to Allison and it will be very difficult for my wife and me. But my mother-in-law is insistent and she's quite able to pay for your services without my help, so I suppose there's not much I can do to prevent it."

"Darren, I know you're upset, but that's no reason to be rude. After all, Sam's here at my request."

"I realize that, Ethel, that's what I'm talking about." He looked at her as though thinking her a silly old woman with more money than good sense.

"You promised you would cooperate, Darren, for my sake." Ethel was on the verge of tears.

"And I will," he said impatiently. He handed me his card. "Please call me, Ms. Hope, if you have any questions for my wife or me. And now, you must excuse us, there are people leaving that we must say goodbye to." With that, he put his hand under his wife's elbow and led her away.

"I'm sorry, Sam," Ethel fussed. "He's just not himself. Allison was their only child and I'm afraid it has just begun to sink in that she's gone. This is a difficult time for all of us. I hope you won't allow his rudeness to deter you. I want to know what happened to my granddaughter."

"Don't worry, Ethel." I patted her arm. "I have no intention of letting him keep me from doing what I can to help. I've made arrangements to meet with Melissa tomorrow and I'll be calling on your daughter and son-in-law soon. I'll give them a few days before imposing but their help will be needed if I'm going to find out anything. They are the only ones who can tell me important details about Allison's disappearance. And now, I must be going."

"Keep in touch, Sam, and if there's anything you need from me, be sure to call."

Gabby was still talking to Mabel, but when she saw me start toward her, she gave Mabel a hug and came to meet me. "Are you ready to go?"

"Yes, let's get out of here. Boy, the girl's father is a real cold fish. Did you meet him?"

"No. But I saw you talking to him and Mrs. Gillespie. He didn't seem too pleased with whatever was being said."

"He doesn't think his mother-in-law should be spending money on an investigation into Allison's death. I suppose he's willing to accept the police finding of suicide or accidental death. Why would a father be so quick to accept a daughter's suicide? You would think he'd want to know for sure what happened." We had reached the van and I opened the door on Gabby's side before going around to the driver's side and jumping in. "By the way, there was someone at the funeral I never would have expected to see. Remember I told you about the guy I was following? The one who caught me in the act? Glen Peters? Well, he and his wife are here. Mabel didn't seem to know them. I wonder what their connection is to the Gillespie family?"

"Perhaps they're neighbors. Maybe you can ask the Gillespies when you see them. You *are* planning to talk to them, aren't you?"

"Yes, but I don't expect much cooperation."

We drove the rest of the way home in silence. As we pulled up to the house, Jill's older daughter, Elisabeth, was going into their apartment and I remembered Jill saying Elisabeth had known Allison slightly. I'd have to talk to her and see if she could shed any light on Allison's life or death. But I'd had enough for one day. I wanted to get out of my dreary clothes and into something casual. I proposed a walk to Gabby. The rain had let up somewhat, but there was still a stiff breeze. The ocean would be wild and rough, just the way I liked it. My idea was greeted with great enthusiasm, especially by Clem and Mimi, who, as soon as they heard the word *walk,* began to dance and race up and down the hall, barking and yelping excitedly. They helped restore our humor and put the day into perspective. Life was for the living and too short to waste a moment.

That night the Psychic Circle met as usual in the living room while I vanished upstairs, using the time to think about what I wanted to ask Melissa when we met the following afternoon. When everyone had gone home and Gabby came upstairs, I asked how the evening had gone.

"It was fine," she said thoughtfully. "After our meditation, we talked for a while about how we might be able to assist in the investigation of Allison's death."

"And what did you conclude?" I thought I'd done

an admirable job of concealing my skepticism, but apparently not.

"Sam, for heaven's sake, don't use that high-and-mighty tone. I know you're not a believer, but that doesn't mean the group can't try to see what it can learn from the spirit world. You don't have to worry that it places any obligation on you, or that we'll interfere with your investigation. Even though I know you think it's all a bunch of hooey, if we come up with anything, I'll let you know. You can use the information or ignore it as you see fit," she concluded, huffing and puffing like the big, bad wolf when he came up against the three little pigs. She turned and walked out.

"Sorry, Gab," I called after her. "I'm not trying to ridicule the group. It's just that I don't see how you can possibly help. But feel free to pass on any messages from out there." I gestured out the window at the stars, which were now bright in the sky, the wind having chased away the few remaining clouds.

As I stood looking at the heavens, I remembered when I was a kid, my mother used to tell me that stars were the souls of people who'd gone to heaven. I wondered if there was one more star in the sky than there had been a few days ago. *Shine brightly, Allison.*

Chapter Six

Melissa Egglington, surrounded by a crowd of friends, was waiting when I pulled up in front of the West Saanich Secondary School at three-thirty the next afternoon. As I stopped the van, they scattered like leaves in the wind and left her alone. Reaching over, I unlocked the door and she climbed in, giving me a hesitant smile.

"Hi, Melissa, how are you today?"

"Okay," she said, ditching the smile and looking glum. She was dressed in black from head to toe and had used black lipstick, which, considering the whiteness of her skin, made her look rather like a ghoul.

"It must be hard, losing your best friend, but trust me, it will get easier after a while."

"What do you know? Allison and I were really close," she said, challenging me to refute her statement.

"I know." I pulled out of the parking spot in front of the school thinking this wasn't going to be easy. Some kids have a chip on their shoulder the size of a tree stump. "Where should we go?"

"I don't know. We usually go to Harry's Café after school, but it will be crowded. Maybe we should go somewhere where it won't be so noisy."

"Are you hungry? I could use a burger. There's a little place not far from here where they make great cheeseburgers and fries."

"Okay."

Such enthusiasm. I could understand her feelings, though, so I decided to ignore her bad humor and pretend all was well. A couple of turns later and we were headed toward the nearest strip mall where I knew a small burger joint. The food was good, and it wouldn't be busy. There certainly wouldn't be any danger of running into the high school crowd either.

Melissa was silent, so I left her to her thoughts and concentrated on my driving. Within a few minutes we were pulling up in front of the café. Lil's had red-checkered curtains on the windows. We went inside and looked around for a good place to sit.

"Brilliant!" Melissa spotted the old jukebox in the corner of the restaurant and headed over to have a closer look. She wouldn't recognize most of the artists and their music because the tunes were mostly rock-and-roll from the sixties and seventies, long before she was born. That's why I liked coming here, it was a trip down memory lane.

"Do you want to try it out?" I asked. Handing her a couple of quarters, I left her to choose some music while I sat down in a corner booth. She joined me just as an old Beatles song started playing. "I highly recommend the cheeseburgers here. They're really good and they come with homemade fries. What do you say?"

She nodded. Boy, this was hard work. She had retreated into her shell again and looked on the verge of tears. We sat silently listening to the music while Lil turned our burgers on the grill and watched us through the window where the orders were placed. When the burgers arrived, Lil had put an extra pickle slice on top of them. They looked as though they were smiling. Even Melissa had to struggle to keep her face grim.

"You know, Allison wouldn't want you to stop enjoying life, Melissa," I chided her gently.

"How do you know?" she asked defensively. "Did you ever meet her?"

"No, but her grandmother has told me how full of life she was. If the tables were turned, would you want her to stop living just because you weren't there?"

"No." She hesitated. "But I feel guilty when I think about her being gone and me still here."

"That's normal." I reached out to pat her arm. "You're going to feel strange for a little while, but pretty soon you'll be able to think about the good times you shared and you'll begin to enjoy life again."

"It's not fair. Why did she have to die?" Tears welled up in her big blue eyes again, threatening to spill over and cause her makeup to run.

"I don't know, but I *do* know that life isn't always fair." I didn't think she expected me to have any answers. I took the opportunity to bring the conversation around to where I wanted it. "Allison's grandmother asked me to try to answer some questions surrounding her death. Will you help me?"

"I guess so. But I don't know anything." She hesitated, then continued. "One day she was around and the next day she wasn't."

"Let's start there then." I pulled out my notebook and opened it. "I'm going to write down everything we talk about. It might help us discover why Allison died. Now, when was the last time you saw her alive?"

She finished her burger and pushed the plate away. "It was Saturday, March first, after supper. She was staying at my place for a couple of days. She went out on a baby-sitting job. I remember the date because we'd had a surprise math test at school a couple of days before, Wednesday, and we both bombed. Allison's parents were really mad at her. Well, just her dad really; her mom never said much. Anyway, when she got to school on Friday, she told me he'd grounded her for the first two weeks of March. She was really mad. She said she was going to run away. She asked if she could stay at my place for a couple of days."

"Did she stay with you often?"

"Yeah, and sometimes I stayed with her." She shrugged as if this was normal behavior. "We spent a lot of time together. But I didn't run away like she did. My parents are pretty cool. She was always fighting with her dad. He's so demanding, always mad about something. Every so often she'd come and stay with me, she called it time-out. When things cooled off, she'd go home."

So that was why Allison's parents hadn't been worried when she hadn't come home and why they hadn't wanted to call the police. They probably thought she was with Melissa.

"So she *was* with you, at least in the beginning."

"But then she disappeared. I thought she'd gone home, until she didn't show up at school on Monday. Then I started getting worried."

"Let me make sure I've got this straight. She was at school on the twenty-eighth, and came to stay with you that night?"

"That's right. We hung out at the mall on Saturday. She had a baby-sitting job on Saturday night, and I went out with my boyfriend. I got home late, about two in the morning." She blushed. "Allison wasn't there. I thought she had gone home to her place from the Peterses' house, but when she—"

"Wait a minute, the Peterses? Who are they?"

"Mr. and Mrs. Peters. They live near Allison's place. She baby-sat for them all the time."

So *that* was the connection between Glen Peters and Allison Gillespie. Strange turn of events—Peters may have been the last person to see Allison alive.

"What happened next?"

"The next day, I called Allison at home, and her mom told me she wasn't there and they hadn't seen her since Friday morning. At first, I didn't worry too much. I thought she might be with Rob, her boyfriend. I didn't say anything to her mom because I didn't want her to know about Rob. But on Monday when she wasn't at school, I got really bummed out. Rob wasn't there either. He hasn't been at school since Allison disappeared. He didn't even show up for her funeral."

Melissa fidgeted in her seat, as if uncomfortable to be revealing this information.

"Do you have any idea where he might be?" I detected a slight hesitation before she replied.

"No, I called his parents and they said he's gone away. I didn't want to seem nosy so I didn't ask where."

"Melissa." I leaned toward her, elbows on the table. "Did the police talk to you after they found Allison? You know, ask you when you last saw her, if she was upset or depressed, that kind of thing?"

"Yeah, but I didn't tell them much," she said, a little of that defensiveness creeping in again. "I just said she wasn't depressed and there's no way she would have killed herself."

"Do they know about Rob being gone or that she even had a boyfriend?"

"I don't know. Allison's parents didn't know about Rob. Her dad thought she was too young to go out with guys so when she and Rob started going out, she didn't tell them." She gave me a worried look. "You won't say anything, will you?"

"Not now, there's no point. I won't say anything unless it becomes important to the investigation. But I'd sure like to talk to him. He may know something, he may have seen Allison after you. If he contacts you please let me know. What's his last name?"

"His name is Reynolds." I asked for his phone number and she gave it to me.

"Do you have any idea why he might have gone away?"

"No." Again she hesitated. "Unless he's really bummed about Allison and needs to chill out."

"You don't think he had anything to do with her death, do you?"

"No way, man! Robbie's a great guy, no way!"

Did she protest a bit too much? "Okay, can you think of anyone who might have wanted to harm Allison? If you don't think it was suicide, what about murder?"

"Murder?" She started, her eyes widening as if she hadn't considered the possibility of murder. A look of fear came over her face. "I don't know. I thought perhaps an accident . . . ?" Her voice trailed off as she grappled with the idea that Allison could have been murdered. Her eyes filled with tears again. "I guess an accident's not too likely. After all, what would she have been doing out at Elk Lake by herself?"

"I don't know. I was hoping you might be able to shed some light on that. Was the lake a hangout for couples or kids who wanted to party?"

"Not that I know of."

"By the way, Melissa, was Allison into drugs? Please be straight with me. I'm not going to judge you or her by your answer, but it will help me to understand what may have happened."

"I don't think so. We never did drugs together; I'm not into that scene and we were together most of the time. I think I would have known."

"What about drinking? Her grandmother seemed to think she didn't drink."

She looked at me sheepishly. "We drank a little at parties but it wasn't a regular thing, just on weekends.

You won't say anything, will you?" she added hurriedly, looking as though she wanted to bolt.

"Don't worry, I'm not about to go running to your parents, or hers. And I won't say anything to her grandmother either. She's got enough to deal with." I closed my notebook. "I guess I should get you home."

"Yeah sure, just drop me back at the school. I don't live far from there."

"Thanks, Melissa. If you think of anything that might help me find out more about Allison, will you call?" I gave her one of my new cards and she looked suitably impressed.

We returned to the school and she got out of the van, turning to thank me for the burger. Just before I drove off, she added, "I'm glad you're looking into Allison's death. Maybe it'll make it easier if I know what happened. I'll try to help. I'll ask some questions around school."

"Thanks, Melissa. And if you need someone to talk to, I'm a pretty good listener."

She walked away, turned back once to wave, then disappeared around a corner. I started the van and drove home.

"So, that's what I found out from Melissa. Not much to go on," I said to Gabby as we sat at the dinner table. Even though I had eaten a burger and fries earlier, I didn't turn down the enchiladas she had ready. As we ate, I told her all about my conversation with Melissa, hoping she'd spot something I'd missed.

"The only thing I can think of is that you need to find Rob. It's curious he would disappear the same time as Allison. There are several possibilities. Perhaps he's feeling depressed over Allison's death and his parents sent him away. Or I suppose he could be implicated in her death and they're trying to protect him or hide him from the police." She frowned. "Maybe he knows something about what happened to Allison and is afraid."

"He could even be dead and his body just hasn't been discovered yet," I added.

Gabby shivered as she sat back and considered the possibilities. "Perhaps there's nothing sinister about his absence—it could have been planned before Allison died. Whatever the reason, it would help if you could find him and have a little chat. Why don't you concentrate your efforts there?"

"I certainly intend to contact his parents, but there are a few other people I need to see—Allison's parents for starters. I also want to talk to Glen Peters. Hopefully he won't recognize me from our little run-in at the warehouse. I have enough to do to keep busy for the next couple of days."

"Is Bill helping? I really don't like the idea of you going to see that Peters guy by yourself."

"Don't worry, I'll be fine," I said, dismissing her concern. "Bill's got a couple of other cases on the go at the moment. If I feel I need help I'll get it."

"The trouble is you never feel like you need anyone's help," she said in an exasperated tone.

"What do you mean?" I asked, picking up on the undercurrent in her voice. "Is this about your Psychic Circle again? I told you I'd listen to whatever you came up with, but you and I just don't happen to see eye to eye on the New Age stuff."

"A little support on things that are important to me would be nice." With that she got up and left me alone in the kitchen to do the dishes and mull over what she'd said.

Chapter Seven

Saturday after breakfast, I called Allison's parents and arranged to see them Monday morning. I didn't want to intrude on their grief, but wanted to at least touch base with them before digging into her life. Once the meeting was arranged, I decided the best approach with Glen Peters would be to show up on his doorstep—I would stop and see him on Monday while in the area. As for Rob's parents, I called but there was no answer. I would keep trying over the weekend.

While upstairs in the office, I called my father. Since our reunion a few months before, I'd tried to establish regular contact and to include him in my life. He and his wife had visited and I'd been to Vancouver to see them. He'd asked me a few times to approach my sister, Martha, to see if she'd be willing to meet him. So far she'd said no each time I broached the subject. When I talked to him that morning, he asked again if she'd changed her mind. Once more I had to answer no, and felt miserable hearing the disappointment in his voice.

"I'll try again, Dad. I'm going to see Martha this week and I'll talk to her again."

"Thanks Sam, I know you'll do what you can."

As soon as I hung up, I got Martha on the phone.

"Marth, it's me."

"Oh, hi Sam. How are you? How's business?" She was skeptical about my prospects as a private investigator and possibly a little jealous I was doing something I wanted to do instead of what I should. Martha was a great one for acting responsibly and wanted the rest of the world to do likewise.

"Great, I'm working on a big case right now. I'll tell you all about it when I see you. Are we still on for lunch this week? Just you and me?"

"Yes, Tuesday isn't it? At noon?"

"Yeah, do you want me to pick you up? Or should we meet downtown?"

"Let's try for downtown. How about that place you're always talking about, The Purple Cabbage?"

"Okay, see you there." I hung up, then tried the Reynolds house again.

"Hello?" This time a woman answered.

"Mrs. Reynolds?"

"Yes?"

"Is Rob home?"

"He's not here," she said abruptly.

"Will he be in later?"

"I'm not sure. Who's calling?"

"My name is Samantha Hope. I'm a friend of Mrs. Beauchamp, Allison Gillespie's grandmother. She asked me to look into events surrounding her granddaughter's death. I understand Rob and Allison were good friends."

"Yes, that's right. We were very sorry to hear about Allison. She was a nice girl, always so polite when she came to the house."

"I was hoping to talk to Rob. I wanted to ask him when he'd last seen or spoken to Allison. I'm trying to retrace her steps those final days."

"Rob was very upset by Allison's death. We've sent him to visit family for a few days. Would you like him to call when he returns?"

I had the distinct impression she was just being polite and wouldn't bother to pass on my message, but said yes anyway and gave her my numbers at work and home, just in case. "If you're talking to Rob, perhaps you could ask him to call me from wherever he is. It's quite urgent that I speak with him as soon as possible."

"I'll tell him. Good-bye."

I didn't bother to say good-bye since she'd already hung up. Clearly, she was very uneasy. I didn't expect to hear from him.

Next I called Ethel Beauchamp to give her a verbal report on my activities and to see if she had heard anything. There was nothing new. She urged me again to try to get to the bottom of the mystery surrounding Allison's death and I promised, again, to do what I could.

* * *

Monday I got into the office early to talk to Bill before going to see the Gillespies. He came in around nine, and we sat down with our coffee and doughnuts, which had become something of a ritual.

"So, fill me in on what's happening with the Beauchamp file, Sam. Are you making any headway?"

"So far, I've just been doing the grunt work, talking to people, trying to get a feel for Allison's life. There are one or two strange twists. You remember that guy, Glen Peters? That insurance report I did?"

"Yeah, what about him? What's he got to do with the girl?"

"Strangely enough, quite a bit. He was at the funeral with his wife the other day and I found out from Allison's friend, Melissa, that Allison used to baby-sit for them all the time. Coincidence?"

"Well, stranger things have happened. Contrary to popular belief, there are such things as coincidences, not everything in life is preordained."

"Don't let Gabby hear you say that," I joked.

"Are you going to have a chat with him?"

"Yes. Oh, there's something else. Allison's boyfriend, Rob Reynolds, has disappeared. His mother says he was overcome with grief and they sent him away to visit family. I think it's kind of unusual he would just leave town like that. No one's seen him since Allison's body was discovered."

"Now that *is* strange. Nose around a little and see what you can find out about him. I wonder if the police know about him?" he mused.

"Melissa's going to ask around at school, and I'll

keep after his parents to see if I can't get them to agree to let me talk to him. I'm off to see Allison's parents this morning. Then I plan to mosey over to the Peters residence and have a chat with Glen. Sure hope he doesn't recognize me."

"Why would he?" Bill looked puzzled.

"Oh, I forgot, I never got around to telling you what happened when I was working on that insurance file." I proceeded to fill him in on how I'd been discovered while watching Glen and his buddies load the truck at the warehouse.

"Maybe *I* should interview Peters," Bill suggested.

"I don't think that's necessary," I said quickly. No way I wanted Bill jumping into my investigation, acting as if I wasn't able to handle it. "If he says anything about recognizing me, I'll just pass it off as another of those coincidences. By the way, what are you up to at the moment?"

"I had a call from a friend who works for Elite Insurance. They had a claim filed by someone who'd been in an accident. Everything looked legit, until they had an anonymous call from a 'concerned citizen'; those are the worst kind. The person seemed to think the claimant had staged his own accident. So my buddy asked me to look into it."

"And what do you think?"

"Too early to tell, but apparently the guy has been switching companies regularly for his optional insurance coverage and has had several claims over the past few years. It certainly looks suspicious."

We parted on that note and I headed out to Saanich for my ten-thirty appointment with the Gillespies.

It was a nice, upscale neighborhood, a newish subdivision with large homes, manicured lawns, and two- or three-car garages. The area looked to be mostly occupied by young or middle-aged professionals, living in homes far too large for the size of their families, the homes being used first and foremost as investments or hedges against inflation.

When I pushed the doorbell there was a corresponding chime that sounded more like Big Ben than a doorbell. It was a few moments before the door opened. I wasn't looking forward to the interview. The Gillespies had been cold and distant when we met at the funeral. *Give them a break, Sam,* I chided myself. After all, they *had* just buried their only child.

"Hello, it's Samantha, isn't it?" Mrs. Gillespie stood inside looking out at me as though I were a stray cat she'd caught digging in her perfect flowerbeds.

"Yes, but please call me Sam." I held out my hand and once again she touched it briefly before she withdrew hers and wiped it surreptitiously on her pant leg.

"Won't you come in?" She was tall and willowy to the point of gauntness, with auburn hair cut in a shoulder-length bob. She had dressed up for our interview or perhaps she always looked this immaculate, in a somber blue silk pantsuit. Her makeup had been applied carefully in an attempt to disguise the fact she'd been crying. That was a good sign. Maybe she wasn't as cold and unfeeling as she first appeared. Today her eyes looked clear and alert—no drugs.

She led me past the living room, which although it could have graced the pages of a home decorating magazine, was cold and sterile. I followed, glancing into the rooms as we passed. There was nothing out of place at all, no sign of life. Finally she gestured for me to enter a small room just off the kitchen, a family room of sorts, where her husband sat reading the paper.

"Darren, this is Samantha—Sam Hope."

"Yes, I remember." He stood, reluctantly, eyeing his newspaper, not pleased to be interrupted. "Please sit down, Ms. Hope. Can I offer you some coffee? I believe my wife has some prepared." He looked at her for confirmation.

"Yes, it should be ready."

"If it's no trouble, that would be nice. With cream, please." I sat in an easy chair opposite the couch where Darren Gillespie was seated, leaving the spot next to him for his wife. He said nothing until she returned with the coffee, setting it on the table between him and me. She poured three cups, put a drop of cream in mine, and handed it to me. She then gave a cup to her husband and took her own, sitting down next to him. After taking a tiny sip, she put down her cup and folded her hands in her lap.

"I see you have a notebook, Ms. Hope. Do you have questions prepared?" His formality was off-putting, but I decided to blunder on, with or without his cooperation, and opened my book.

"I thought perhaps you and Mrs. Gillespie could tell me about Allison. I never had the pleasure of meeting her, so it would be helpful."

Mrs. Gillespie hesitated, waiting for her husband to take the lead.

"Allison was a beautiful, bright, young teenager.

She did well in school, excelled at sports, and had many friends. She was well liked by everyone. In the past couple of years, she had begun acting out. She had become rebellious and cheeky and had started skipping classes. No doubt had she lived, she would have outgrown this unpleasant phase and become a responsible young adult. Now she won't have the chance."

"Do you have any idea what was behind Allison's rebellion? Was she having problems at school? Was it the influence of not-so-desirable friends?"

"I blame my wife entirely for Allison's childish behavior," Darren said. "Judy spoiled Allison from the beginning, allowing her to have her own way when she should have kept tighter discipline. My work takes me away from home frequently so I have not always been here to see to these matters myself."

I glanced at Mrs. Gillespie, a little nonplussed that her husband would make such a harsh statement, especially in front of me, a total stranger. She had blanched and her hands fidgeted nervously with a handkerchief that she'd taken out of her pocket.

"Darren, I don't think that's fair—" she tried to interject, but he silenced her with a scathing look.

"Judy, we've been over this before," he said firmly, closing the subject.

"When did you last see Allison alive?"

"My wife can answer that question for you," he said, giving her permission to speak.

"It was Friday, the last day of February. She got up and left for school as usual and that was the last time

I saw her." She looked on the verge of tears but kept her grip on the handkerchief and her eyes stayed dry.

"Did you have any reason to suspect that she might not have been planning to come home?"

"No, not really, I just remember she had her knapsack on her shoulder but she always took it to school. She gave me a hug and kiss before she left." She dabbed at her eyes then, glancing at her husband, sat up straight and rigid, bringing herself under control.

"What about you, Mr. Gillespie?"

"What do you mean?" He looked uneasy and for a moment I thought his iron grip might be weakening.

"When did you last see Allison?"

"It was the Thursday night. I had already gone to work on Friday morning before she got up."

"And did anything happen which might give us a clue as to why Allison decided to run away?"

"Run away? Who said Allison ran away?"

"Her grandmother and her friend, Melissa . . ." I left my sentence dangling to see if he'd bite.

"Yes, well, she has run away in the past, but I'm not sure that's what happened this time," he said, hedging a little. He had no idea I knew that he and Allison had quarreled the night before she left.

"Was there a disagreement of any kind?"

"Why do you ask?"

"Mr. Gillepsie, the police have indicated they don't suspect foul play in Allison's death. That would indicate either an accident or that Allison took her own life. Did she have any reason to be upset or depressed?"

"No, she didn't. Allison didn't commit suicide," he

stated emphatically, leaving no room for argument. "Her death was an accident caused by irresponsible behavior. The autopsy showed Allison had been drinking. She was unaccustomed to alcohol. She may have gone to the lake with some of her friends. They were probably all drinking; Allison must have fallen into the water and drowned and the rest of them got frightened and ran away. Now they won't come forward and say what really happened for fear they'll get into trouble. That's what's wrong with young people these days—total lack of responsibility."

"Darren, I don't think—"

"Judith, that's right, you don't think." Gillespie cut his wife off as though he didn't want her contradicting him.

He had obviously decided to give everyone the impression that she was entirely responsible for Allison's death and he'd had no part in it. He hadn't admitted there had been a disagreement between he and Allison the night before she ran away and seemed to want to blame his wife or Allison's friends for everything. I wasn't going to get any more out of him and as for Mrs. Gillespie, she wouldn't talk as long as he was sitting next to her. I closed my notebook and stood up.

"Thanks for your help. If I think of anything else I need to know, I hope you won't mind me calling again."

Now that he could see the interview was over and I was leaving, Darren Gillespie decided to be polite. It was as though the whole exercise had been a game to him and since he hadn't revealed anything important, he was the winner and could afford to be magnanimous.

"Of course not. Ms. Hope, I wouldn't like to leave you with the impression that we didn't care about Allison. We did. But I'm not in agreement with my mother-in-law about having Allison's death investigated further. The police have made their ruling and I am satisfied that if there were anything untoward, they would have discovered it. I hope you won't be offended if I say that my mother-in-law is laboring under the delusion that somehow you will find something startling that will explain why Allison died. But nothing will bring her back, so how can this make a difference?"

"You're right of course, nothing will bring her back. But it may bring some comfort to Allison's grandmother and friends if we are able to discover how she died. There's a cloud hanging over the matter, as long as people think that she may have committed suicide or that someone else may have been involved. No one should have to shoulder guilt or feel they could have prevented her death if it was at all possible. And if foul play *was* involved, the person responsible should not remain at large. Thank you for your time. I'll be in touch." I started toward the door and Mrs. Gillespie followed.

"Let me show you out."

"Thanks." When we were out of earshot of the ogre, I said to Judy, "I feel as though you and I haven't really had a chance to talk. Would you mind if I called you again sometime?"

She said, "I don't think that would be wise. Why

don't you give me your card and I'll call you." I took that to mean she was willing to talk, but not when her husband was around, so I gave her the card and said, "Call anytime."

Just then I remembered I had forgotten to ask the Gillespies what they knew about Glen Peters and his wife.

"By the way, Judy, I understand Allison baby-sat for the Peters family on a regular basis. Melissa told me Allison was baby-sitting the Saturday night before she disappeared. Do you know anything about them?"

"No." She hesitated. "Allison baby-sat there often—once or twice a week. Her father thought she should earn her own spending money." Eyes downcast, she picked at her slacks, twisting the material into a ball.

"How did she meet the Peterses? Are they family friends?"

"No, we had never met them until the day of Allison's funeral. I believe one of her girlfriends referred her to them. It might even have been Melissa."

"Okay, thanks. I'll look forward to hearing from you."

"Thank you, Sam." She gave me a sad little smile and stood at the door, watching as I drove off.

I was beginning to get a picture of what life was like for Allison. She'd had all the material things money could buy—but where was the love and affection, the spontaneity? With a rigid disciplinarian for a father and a mother who was afraid of her own shadow, she hadn't stood a chance. Strange her father hadn't wanted to admit she'd run away or that they had fought. It was as though he thought doing so might lay his relationship with his daughter open to scrutiny. He might even have to accept some responsibility for what had happened. That would never do.

Chapter Eight

My stomach was sending a clear message that it was time for lunch. I didn't want to drive all the way home and then back to Saanich to see Peters, so I headed for Lil's. I got the last booth, plunked myself down, and looked around for the server. I always ordered a cheeseburger, fries, and a vanilla shake so I didn't need to look at the menu. Giving my order to the first employee that passed my booth, I settled back to indulge in my favorite occupation—people watching. The crowd at Lil's was my age or older. There were a few suits, but most of the clientele were dressed casually, laborers or tradespeople on their lunch breaks. Lil's was like a truck stop without the trucks. People could get good wholesome food like burgers, fries, and homemade slaw at reasonable prices. The service was quick and efficient and the coffeepot bottomless.

In no time, my burger was sitting in front of me, the pickle smiling up from its place of honor, and the fries crisp and brown. I slathered the fries with ketchup and dug in. For some reason, Lil's burgers tasted even better for being somewhat illicit. Gabby had been trying for some time to convert me to vegetarianism and I had agreed to try it. This wasn't the kind of place Gabby and I could ever visit together. She would find nothing on the menu to enjoy; even the salads were made from iceberg lettuce rather than the gourmet stuff she liked. I sighed to think this was a part of my life she would never share, but then some pleasures are better enjoyed solo anyway.

After several cups of coffee and a trip to the ladies room, I paid my bill, left a hefty tip, and went back out to the van feeling considerably heavier than when I'd arrived. I really wanted to go home and take a nap, but the feeling would pass when I got to the Peters residence.

I drove the short distance back to Saanich and found the house. There was no sign of life, but a battered station wagon was parked in the driveway. It must be Peters's own vehicle back from the body shop. The back of the vehicle looked freshly painted and conspicuous compared to the rest, which was scratched and dented. I got out of the van, locked the door, and made my way past a small two-wheeler with a set of training wheels and a deflated soccer ball lying on the grass next to the sidewalk. I rang the doorbell, then heard footsteps approaching. My heart pounded as I waited for the door to open. Would he recognize me?

"Hello." A pleasant young woman whom I recognized as Mrs. Peters smiled at me while her young son peeked out from behind her legs.

"Hi, my name is Samantha Hope. I wonder if I might ask you a few questions about Allison Gillespie?"

"Allison? Oh, yes, Allison, our baby-sitter. That was a terrible tragedy, wasn't it? Are you family?"

"No, I'm a friend of Allison's grandmother. She asked me to talk to people that Allison may have been in contact with. I understand she may have been baby-sitting for you and your husband on the Saturday before she died."

"When would that have been? She was here often."

"March first, I believe."

"I would have to look at my calendar." She stopped, then continued, "Oh, I'm forgetting my manners. Won't you come in? Would you like some coffee or tea?" She scooped up her son and balanced him on her hip.

"Whatever you're having," I said, wondering where I'd put it.

"Coffee then." She led the way to the kitchen. As I rounded the corner, I started. Peters was sitting at the kitchen table, reading a magazine.

"Glen, this is Samantha Hope. She wants to ask us some questions about Allison." Now it was his turn to look startled. He glanced up quickly, his eyes betraying his wariness. Then just as quickly he looked back down at his magazine. He carefully closed it and looked up again, this time with studied indifference.

"I was saying to Mrs. Peters—"

She interjected, "Trudy, please."

"—to Trudy, that Mrs. Beauchamp, Allison's grandmother, has asked me to speak to Allison's friends and anyone else who may have seen her during the last few days before she died."

"Glen, do you remember if we had Allison here to baby-sit on March first?" Trudy interrupted.

"I don't know offhand, but take a look at the calendar. I know you write everything down," he teased his wife.

She went off to find her calendar, leaving me alone in the kitchen with him. He motioned for me to sit opposite him and poured me a mug of coffee. He was tall and slim with dark hair and eyes. He hadn't shaved and the day or two's growth of beard gave him a slightly seedy look, as though he'd been partying the night before and gotten up with a nasty hangover.

I busied myself with my coffee, then as I looked up, caught him studying me as intently as I had been studying him a moment ago.

"Say, you look kinda familiar. Have we met?" he asked suggestively as if flirting.

"I don't think so, unless perhaps you noticed me at Allison's funeral. I remember seeing you there." I put a note of admiration in my voice, as though I'd been impressed by his good looks. I was trying desperately to distract him from recalling our confrontation down by the warehouse.

"I don't think that's it." He frowned. "I'm usually pretty good at remembering faces. Oh well, I'm sure it will come to me."

Boy, I hope not.

"I found it." Trudy walked back into the kitchen

waving a calendar. "I put Tommy down for his nap," she said in an aside to her husband. "Allison did sit for us that night. Remember, we went over to Nick and Trish's to play cards?"

"Oh, right," he answered quickly.

"Do you recall what time Allison left here?"

"Well." Trudy hesitated, appearing to consider the question. "I think we got home around midnight. Glen offered to drive her home as usual, but she said not to bother, she'd call her boyfriend. She used the phone and then about ten minutes later, she looked out the front room window, said good-bye, and left. I assumed her boyfriend was outside."

"So you didn't see him yourself?"

"No, I never even looked. It wasn't the first time he'd come to pick her up."

"Did she seem upset or depressed at all?"

"No, she was the same old Allison. She was always great with Tommy. He can be quite a handful. But he loved her. She was always thinking up new games to play with him and she was firm but fair. He was devoted to her."

"So you don't have any idea what happened to her?"

"No, none whatever. She was fine when she left here at midnight, Saturday. We didn't know she'd had a fight with her father and wasn't planning on going home until we talked to Melissa at the funeral." She glanced quickly at her husband, realizing that what she had just said confirmed she and Peters had known very well that Allison had been baby-sitting for them that Saturday, long before I showed up asking questions.

"She mentioned that Allison had not been seen since Saturday," she added quickly.

If they'd spoken to Melissa at the funeral, why did they make such a production of pretending to not know if Allison had been at their house on the Saturday before her death? They must know Saturday night may have been the last time she'd been seen alive.

"Thanks a lot for your help." I drained my coffee cup and got up to leave. "If you think of anything else I should know, please call." I handed my card to Trudy.

"For sure," Glen said. He waved as Trudy led me back to the door.

"Sorry we couldn't help. I'll call if we think of anything important."

"Thanks." I jumped in the van, started it, and drove off quickly, almost hitting a car that had been parked in front of me and decided to pull out at the same time. I leaned on the horn and two men in the other vehicle, a dark, late-model Ford, turned to give me dirty looks. As I caught a glimpse of their faces, my nerves jumped. I recognized one of them. The driver, who had short blond hair and a big mouth that was poised to yell at me, spotted me the same time I eyeballed him. He was a guy I'd met a few times at parties at Bill's place when he was still on the force. He was a plainclothes cop. What the heck was he doing in front of the Peters place? The Ford pulled up to the stop sign at the corner and he jumped out of his vehicle and walked quickly toward the van.

"Sam, what the heck?"

"Hello, Trevor, nice to see you, too!"

"Sorry, but you're the last person I expected to see coming out of *that* place."

"Well, I wasn't exactly expecting to see you either." A horn honked behind me and we realized we were blocking traffic.

"Meet me at McDonald's, the one at the corner of Vancouver and Pandora downtown. I'll buy you a coffee. We need to talk."

"We do?" I asked innocently.

"Yes, we do. Be there," he said in a voice that forbade disagreement. He walked quickly back to his vehicle and pulled away from the stop sign.

I followed them down the highway into town and when they turned off Blanshard onto Johnston Street, then onto Vancouver, I kept on their tail until they turned into McDonald's. Pulling in behind them, I got out of the van and locked the door. Even with two of Victoria's finest around, I wasn't taking any chances.

Not that anyone would know who they were. Trevor was dressed in faded jeans and an old Irish fisherman's-knit sweater. His partner, no one I knew, had his head shaved and wore an earring in his right ear. He was handsome in a scary kind of way.

Trevor motioned us to an isolated table at the back of the restaurant and we went to sit down while he got the coffee.

"Fraser," the skinhead said, sticking out his hand, which swallowed mine in its grasp. I couldn't help but laugh.

"What's wrong?" he asked gruffly.

"Fraser? I think you need a name change to go with

that getup." I pointed to his black leather vest and haircut.

He smiled sheepishly. "You're right. How do you and Trevor know each other?"

"Let's just say we met through friends."

Trevor picked that moment to come toward us bearing a tray with three coffees and three apple turnovers.

"So, Sam, what gives? What were you doing at the Peters house?"

"You first." I was stubbornly silent.

"Oh, all right," he said in an exasperated tone. "Peters is a suspect in a drug investigation. We're watching his comings and goings. We wanted to see who shows up at his place, if we recognize them, you know the drill. Imagine my surprise at seeing you there. What's your connection to him?"

I didn't know if he knew about Bill and I setting up our own agency so I filled him in on that first, then explained about Allison. "When I saw you, I thought perhaps Allison's file was still open. Thought maybe there were still some loose ends, that perhaps Peters was somehow implicated."

"I didn't know about the girl. I knew a body had been found at Elk Lake, but I heard it was an accident or maybe suicide and that the file had been closed. I don't know if the investigating officer is aware of our interest in Peters or that Allison used to baby-sit his kid. It's probably just a coincidence, but I'll touch base with him."

"Keep me posted on what you find out, please. Allison's grandmother asked me to try to find out what happened to her. She doesn't accept the accident/suicide theory. If you learn anything, I'd like to know."

"Sure." I gave him my card and he dug around in his pockets, then realized he wasn't carrying any. "I'll call you," he promised. "So how are you doing anyway, Sam?"

When Trevor had been hanging around with Bill in their early days on the force, he had tried to hit on me, even though I had told him I wasn't interested. He thought he was my Mr. Right. Granted he *was* good-looking and could be charming—smooth like snake oil—but I hadn't been interested then and still wasn't. Now his partner, Fraser, was another kettle of fish. I don't know if it was the shaved head or the leather, but I found him quite attractive. I gave him my sweetest smile.

"I'm doing just fine."

"So things have worked out okay for you? You're still not interested," he tried to joke, but it was one of those jokes that usually turn out to be more serious than funny. What an ego!

"No, thanks. Besides, I heard you got married." I smiled sweetly.

He had the good grace to blush, like a little kid who's just been caught playing doctor.

"Just kidding, you know that."

"Sure, sure," I replied sarcastically. "Anyway, thanks for the info, and I'll hear from you soon." I got up to leave. "Why don't you drop over some time, with your wife—and bring Fraser along. He's cute!"

I threw my most alluring smile at Fraser, who gave me a look that said "maybe."

I took that as a good omen and headed home to Mimi.

Chapter Nine

Lunch with Martha was always difficult. She was the typical older sister, bossy and a bit of a mother hen. She'd taken me under her wing when we were kids, and although this had its benefits, she'd also tried to stifle my independence, something that still made me want to rebel at everything she and everyone else said.

My plan was to try to get her to take some advice from me for a change. It wasn't going to be easy, because the subject I planned to bring up would raise her hackles.

Martha and Mother had conspired to conceal our parents' divorce. Since I was only two, I had no memories of this time. I'd grown up thinking that Hugo, my mother's second husband, was my father. He was and is a wonderful man and, don't get me wrong, admirably played the role of dad. But when I found out he was actually my stepfather, I was pretty mad that this had been kept a secret.

Now that I had located my birth father, I couldn't understand why Martha wasn't willing to be reunited with him, too.

I got to The Purple Cabbage first and grabbed a booth in the corner next to a window so I could watch for her. She was late, so I amused myself by eating all the carrot and celery sticks and a loaf of the café's excellent homemade bread. I waved when she walked in and came over, sliding onto the seat opposite me.

"Hi, how come you're late? You're never late," I teased. Martha had a reputation; she'd been late for her own wedding and every other important family gathering before and after it.

"Sorry, I had a couple of errands to run and they took longer than expected. Have you been here long?"

"Don't worry about me, I always try to arrive early so I can eat all the bread while I'm waiting." The restaurant was famous for its small French loaves, baked fresh on the premises. "I'll see if they'll bring another loaf." I spotted our waiter and motioned him over. "What would you like to eat?"

"Order me whatever you're having," she said. Martha had never taken much of an interest in food, silly girl. That's why she was willowy and I wasn't.

"We'll have two Caesar salads and another loaf of bread, please."

My strategy was to ply her with good food before introducing the touchy subject of our father. We sat and gossiped while we waited for lunch to arrive, then were quiet as we ate our salads. As the time drew near to bring up the subject, my nerves began to hum. It had never been easy to get Martha to see anything my way; why should this time be any different?

"How is my wonderful nephew, Timothy?"

"Perfect as always. He's trying to sit up by himself now. Steven's at home with him today. I love him to bits, but it's nice to get out of the house for a while and not have to lug his diaper bag and all his paraphernalia along."

"Mom and Dad are lucky to be able to watch their grandson grow up." I chose my words carefully. "There's someone else who'd really like to be part of his life."

"If you're talking about Richard Howell, you might as well forget it," she said stubbornly, sticking out her chin and frowning.

"Martha, hear me out, just this once. Imagine you had a wonderful child like Timmy and you loved him very much. You know how that feels. Now suppose something happened, you got depressed or down on your luck and you start drinking and hanging out with the wrong crowd. Suppose Steven wanted a divorce, and you agreed because you knew you were bad for him. You had a rough few years, quite a few in fact. Then you began to turn your life around. Do you mean to tell me you don't think you would deserve a second chance? We all make mistakes. I'm not saying you have to invite Father for dinner every Sunday, but give him a chance to apologize for the past and meet your family."

She burst into tears and I reached in my bag for a tissue and handed it to her.

"You don't remember what it was like; you were too young. It felt like the end of the world when he walked out of our lives and never came back."

"You're not a little girl anymore. You've got your own family now. He just wants to see you. What about it?"

"I'd feel like such a traitor to Mom."

"He doesn't want to force you to take sides. He just wants to play a small part in your life. Mom is happily remarried and has been for more than thirty years. How can this hurt her?"

"I don't know, but I'm sure she'll feel as though I've deserted her."

"Hugo is wonderful. Talk to him and let him know what you're planning, he'll smooth the way."

"What if he doesn't like me?"

Ah, so that was the problem! "Why wouldn't he?" I gave her an encouraging smile. "You're wonderful! So can I tell him we'll be over soon to visit?"

"Let me think about it. I admit I may have been wrong, but I need time to get used to the idea."

"Okay, but don't wait too long. Too much time has been lost already. Now what about one of those sinfully rich chocolate desserts over there?" I asked, changing the subject quickly before she had second thoughts.

She smiled. "Do you ever stop thinking about your stomach, Sam? Oh, all right, we'll share."

By the end of the lunch Martha had forgiven me and told me to call Richard and arrange a meeting. I was on top of the world as I hurried home, planning how I'd call right away.

But when I let myself into the apartment, I got sidetracked and forgot all about calling. Gabby, a worried look on her face, came rushing out to meet me.

"You had a call while you were out, Sam. It was Mrs. Reynolds. Isn't that Allison's boyfriend Rob's mother? She sounded upset."

"Did she say what she wanted?"

"No, she just asked if you were home and when I said no, she said to have you call as soon as you got in."

I took the stairs two at a time and went to the telephone at my desk. I hadn't expected to hear from her again. I dialed the Reynolds residence.

"Hello."

"Mrs. Reynolds, Sam Hope. You called?"

"Oh, Ms. Hope, thank you for calling back so promptly."

"Please, call me Sam."

"Sam, have you spoken with Rob?"

"No," I said, puzzled. She had said he was away and didn't want him upset. Why did she think I would have spoken to him?

"Oh dear, I hoped he might have called you. I talked to him on Saturday night after you and I spoke and I gave him your message. I'm worried about him."

"What do you mean? I thought you said he was visiting family."

"He was, my husband took him there himself. Rob was very upset by Allison's death. My husband's sister and her family live in Nanaimo. He drove Rob up there to get him away from Victoria and give him a few days to grieve without having to worry about school or anything else. Today we had a call from Roberta. That's my husband's sister. She said Rob had told them he wanted to take the bus back home to Victoria. He should have arrived home last night. She called today to see if he'd made it home safely. We didn't know he was coming. He didn't show up last night and he hasn't called. We don't know where he is." Her voice cracked. "I think he's in some kind of trouble, and after what happened to Allison, I'm worried about him."

I was worried, too. Maybe it was no coincidence that Rob had disappeared. Was there a connection between Allison's death and Rob's disappearance? Considering Allison had turned up dead, it didn't bode well for Rob.

"Have you tried calling his friends?"

"I can't reach anyone. They would still be in school. I have to wait until later this afternoon."

"Have you reported his disappearance to the police?"

She broke down completely. "No, I thought there must be a simple explanation. I kept thinking he'd turn up any minute. But he hasn't, and now I don't know what to think."

"Back up just a little. When did he leave Nanaimo?"

"Yesterday afternoon, Roberta said she and Doug put him on the bus at four o'clock. He should have arrived in Victoria around seven. She didn't call until today because she didn't think there would be a problem. After all, it's not that far, and he *is* sixteen. Then I guess she started thinking and decided she should have alerted us. So she called this morning at ten. We hadn't heard from him. Now she feels terrible and I don't know what to do."

"The first step is to call the school and see if he's there. If he isn't, perhaps you should talk to some of his friends before jumping to conclusions. If no one has seen him, we need to alert the police. I know they have a policy about not declaring someone missing until they've been gone for a certain number of hours, but I don't know exactly what it is. Considering what happened to Allison, I think the circumstances warrant their involvement." I glanced at my watch. Two-thirty. "Why don't you call the school while classes are still in session and see if Rob's there. Perhaps the principal could talk to his friends and find out if they've heard from him."

"I'll do that right now."

"Good. Call me back and let me know what you find out. I'll wait by the phone."

"Thank you, Sam."

" 'Bye." I hung up the phone. Gabby had come into the office and had been listening to the last part of my conversation with Mrs. Reynolds.

"What's happened, Sam?"

"Apparently Rob was staying with his aunt and uncle in Nanaimo. He left there yesterday afternoon on the bus and hasn't turned up at home. His mother is worried sick about him. So am I, for that matter. It doesn't look good."

"You're right, I wonder if there's any way of checking with the bus depot to find out if anyone remembers seeing him get off the bus."

"Perhaps, but it's a long shot. Who would have noticed? I think I'll just wait until Mrs. Reynolds calls me back, and if he wasn't at school we'll try and figure out what to do next. I wonder if he could have gotten spooked when his mother told him I wanted to talk to him about Allison. Maybe he knows something about her death."

We went downstairs and I put on a pot of coffee. When it was ready we sat at the kitchen table, waiting for the phone to ring. I kept looking at my watch every few minutes, until finally Gabby said,

"Sam, that isn't going to make the time go any faster. Why don't you find something to do while you're waiting?"

"You're right, I should find something to do." I began to pace up and down the kitchen. "We're losing precious time. What's taking the woman so long?"

"It's only been an hour. Once she called the school, it would take a while for the principal to try to locate Rob's friends and find out if he was at school. Don't worry; she'll call as soon as she knows something."

Just then the phone rang and I picked it up in the kitchen.

"Sam, Ann Reynolds. Everything's okay. Rob just walked in the door."

"Where the heck was he?" I asked. If I'd been there I would have shaken some sense into the boy, but all I could do was try not to sound too annoyed at his mother for having raised her son to be so irresponsible.

"When he got off the bus last night, he stopped to see a friend. It got late and he didn't want to call for a ride home, so he stayed at his friend's and went to school with him in the morning."

"Why didn't he call and let you know where he was?"

"He didn't think I knew he'd left Nanaimo, so he didn't think I'd be worried. I could ring his neck," she admitted.

"Well, I'm glad everything's all right. Could you ask him if he can meet me tomorrow to talk about Allison?"

"Just a minute."

I waited as she and Rob discussed my request. I could hear their muffled voices but couldn't make out the conversation. She came back on the line.

"Why don't you come to the house after school tomorrow? He'll be here." She gave me the address, which I wrote down.

"I'll see you tomorrow then—is four o'clock okay?"

"That's fine. And Sam, thanks for your help. I feel a little foolish to have made such a fuss."

"Don't. You were right to be concerned. I'm just glad all's well. See you tomorrow." I hung up and turned to Gabby. "If that were my kid, he'd be grounded until he turned twenty-one. Honestly!"

"Never mind. He's safe, that's all that matters."

I grumbled some more but knew Gabby was right. Perhaps his mother and I had overreacted. Worried about Allison's death, I had started imagining all kinds of horrible things, any of which might have happened to him. I should be glad things had turned out okay. He was safe and I'd have a chance to talk to him and find out if he had any idea what had happened to Allison.

When I calmed down, I told Gabby about lunch

with Martha. Then I went upstairs to call my father. I would make time to go with Martha to visit him before too long. He'd be impatient to see her and baby Tim. But he'd waited this long, a few more days wouldn't hurt. I had a few more leads to follow first. I needed to find out what happened to Allison. Maybe my conversation with Rob would move the investigation forward.

Chapter Ten

Rob greeted me with a sheepish grin when I arrived at the Reynolds residence the next afternoon. He was a good-looking kid, and knew it. I could tell his parents had given him a good verbal lashing for his behavior, as he apologized.

"You're Sam. I know because Melissa told me about your spiked hair. She said you'd be wearing a cool leather jacket. I'm sorry if my mom got you worried. I think she overreacted, don't you?"

"I'm on your mom's side, Rob. After what happened to Allison, I think we both had a right to be worried."

At the mention of Allison's name, his face fell and a look of pain replaced the impudent grin. "I'm sorry, you're right. I guess I was a little thoughtless. Come on in. Mom made some coffee and there are fresh ginger cookies. They're still warm."

"Thanks."

I followed him into the kitchen, where the smell of spices permeated the air. His mother had set out coffee mugs and a plate of cookies.

"Hello, Mrs. Reynolds, I'm Sam Hope."

"Sam, I'm Ann." She shook my hand. "Rob, take Sam's jacket and put it in the hall."

I slipped off the jacket and handed it to Rob, who admired the worn leather. It had taken me a few years to get it looking like that. I saw him slip it over his shoulders as he rounded the corner, then stop to admire himself in a full-length mirror in the hallway before putting it down. He came back and sat down at the table, taking a handful of cookies on his way past the plate.

"Rob, offer those to Sam first. Where are your manners?" his mother scolded.

He held the plate out to me and I took a couple, just to put him at ease mind you, then added some cream to the coffee and took a sip. Would it be impolite to dunk? I decided against it and settled for helping myself to another cookie. This was pleasant, but I wasn't there just for the fun of it. I had work to do.

"Rob, thanks for agreeing to talk about Allison. It must be hard. I'm sure you were fond of her."

"Yeah, she was great. You know, the worst thing is she and I had a big fight at the mall on the Saturday before she died and she was really mad at me. We didn't get a chance to patch it up. Next thing I know she's disappeared and then they find her out at the lake. Now it's too late."

"I was going to ask when you had last seen her. You say Saturday afternoon? I understand she was baby-sitting Saturday night. The Peterses told me you picked her up from their place around midnight."

"No, usually when she baby-sat on the weekends I would pick her up and we'd hang out for a while before she went home." He gave his mother a sidelong glance, as if he wasn't keen on discussing his love life in front of her. But she didn't seem surprised, so he continued. "After the fight, she told me not to bother coming to get her. I thought Mr. Peters would give her a ride home or back to Melissa's."

"Mrs. Peters said Allison called someone to come and pick her up. Any idea who she might have called, if not you?"

"No. She always called me, and if I couldn't make it, or if she had to get home early, Mr. Peters gave her a ride."

Hmm, if Rob didn't give her a ride, who did?

"What did you and Allison fight about?"

Rob hesitated and glanced at his mother. With more tact than I would have exhibited had I been in her shoes, Ann excused herself and left the room.

"The parents of one of our friends were away for the weekend and he had asked a few of us to hang out at his place. Word got around the school, and everybody was planning on going. I wanted Allison to cancel on the Peterses and come to the party. She said she couldn't because she'd given her word. I told her I was going without her and she got really mad. I went to the party. Even if Allison had called, I wouldn't have been able to pick her up. I wasn't at home. And

I'd had a few beers besides. Don't tell my mother. She'll freak out."

"I won't say anything. I'm not trying to get anyone in trouble. I just want to know what happened to Allison.

"Was the party near Elk Lake? Allison's dad seemed to think that Allison might have been drinking with friends out at the lake and fallen into the water by accident."

"No, like I said, it was at a friend's place. The police came and broke it up," he admitted guiltily. "All our friends were there, so there's no way Allison could have been drinking with friends at the lake. Besides, no one hangs out there. It's too far away and there's always someone's house available."

"Did Allison do drugs?"

"No way. We had a few drinks sometimes, but we never used dope. She didn't even really like to drink. She just did it once in a while, so the other kids wouldn't think she wasn't cool."

"What do *you* think happened to Allison?"

"I don't know, man. I just hope it wasn't suicide. I keep thinking, maybe if we hadn't had the fight she'd still be alive. I mean, we'd had lots of fights before, but we always made up. I don't think she'd kill herself over a silly fight, do you?" He looked scared.

"No, I don't," I reassured him. "I've talked to Melissa and Allison's grandmother, and neither of them thought that Allison was depressed or would ever consider suicide. Have you thought about what else could have happened?"

"I've been trying to figure it out. Up at my aunt and

uncle's I had lots of time to think. But I just don't know."

"Did Allison ever mention being afraid? Do you think it's possible she might have been murdered?"

"I don't know. I hadn't really thought about murder. The police said an accident or suicide. I kept thinking, maybe she killed herself because of our fight. Pretty self-centered, I guess," he said sheepishly.

"Rob, we don't know what happened yet, but we'll get to the bottom of this. If you think of anything, no matter how insignificant, please call." I gave him my card, and he slipped it into his pocket. "And be careful—if Allison was murdered, that would mean there's someone out there who doesn't want us to know what happened. Don't go around asking too many questions. And don't get your parents all worried again or I will personally come after you," I teased, as his mother peeked her head around the corner.

"All finished?" she asked. "Sorry to interrupt, but I need to get dinner started."

"That's okay," I said, getting up from the table, "we're all donc. Thanks for the coffee and cookies. I'd better get home. Nice to meet you, Ann. Rob, will you show me where you hid my jacket, please? I know you were hoping I'd forget it, but it's a little breezy out there."

"Thanks for your help the other day, Sam," Ann said. "Good luck with your investigation."

I walked quickly to the van and started it up, putting it in reverse and backing out of the driveway. Rob seemed like a nice kid and he had, I thought, been frank. I was more inclined to believe him than Peters when it came to Allison. After all, Peters had tried to cheat the insurance company. He wasn't the most honest guy around. Rob was a better bet. Also, he knew Allison and all her friends. If he said he hadn't picked her up from Peters's because he'd been partying at a friend's house, I believed him. And it shot down Allison's father's theory, too. If all her friends were at a house party, she wasn't at the lake drinking with them. There was more digging to be done before I got to the bottom of this mystery.

When I got home, I filled Gabby in on my conversation with Rob and suggested we take the dogs for a walk after dinner. I wanted to drive to Elk Lake and walk the trail near where Allison's body had been found. Gabby balked, then realized I was going with or without her, and agreed to tag along.

It took twenty minutes to drive to the lake and park the van. The dogs were all excited; they hadn't had much exercise for a couple of days and were ready for a good run. I let them out and they danced around the parking lot, then sat quietly while we fastened on their leashes. We set out around the east side of the lake. The evening was pleasant and cool enough that there weren't many mosquitoes. As soon as we got onto the trail and could see there wasn't much foot traffic, we let the dogs loose. They frolicked around in the leaves and underbrush, and then settled down, Mimi walking beside us, and Clem running ahead. She always had to be in front, leading the way. When she came to a fork in the trail, she waited long enough to see which way we wanted to go and then scampered ahead again.

She stopped and sniffed at all the interesting scents. Every once in a while she disappeared into the brush and we would call her back to keep her in our sights.

"It's great to get out for a walk, don't you think?" I asked Gabby, who was still miffed at me for insisting we come to Elk Lake.

"If you ask me, it's a little spooky," she grumbled.

"You should like that, Gab. Ghosts and beings from the other world. Aren't those the same spirits you're always trying to contact on Thursday nights?"

"Sam, you're a real pain sometimes. You know exactly what I mean. This place is depressing after what happened to Allison."

"I know. But you're safe with me."

"Great," she said sarcastically. "I feel so much better now."

"I just wanted to get a feel for the place." I looked around in the direction we had come from. "We're quite a long way from the car park. What could Allison have been doing way out here? I can't help thinking she wouldn't have come here alone. Imagine what it must be like at night. If you think it's spooky now, I'll bet it would be even worse after dark."

Gabby shivered.

"Hey, where's Clem? She must have wandered into the bush again. Clem?" I called out to her, but she didn't come running as she usually did. Mimi was walking beside Gabby and looked up expectantly. "Clem," I called again. "Where *is* that dog?"

Just then I heard a rustling off to the right. The lake was on our left and a small trail branched to the right. I followed it for a few feet, while Gabby and Mimi waited at the fork. I could see something gray and white up ahead, and knew it must be Clem. But she wasn't responding to my calls. A few more feet and I caught up to her. She was rooting around in the low brush and didn't look up as I approached.

"Clem, come." I advanced closer to have a look. "Clem old girl, what have you found? I couldn't see anything but she obviously had found the scent of another animal. I crouched down and took a look. Something white under the bush caught my eye. Clem finally backed out of the brush and ran back up the trail to Mimi and Gabby. I pushed my way into the spot she had vacated and reached out for the white object. My hand touched something damp and I pulled it out to take a better look. It was just a matchbook cover. There was something written on the front, Waterworks Café, and an address on the back. The A print was small and it was getting dark out, so I couldn't quite make it out. I shoved it in my pocket to examine later.

"Sam, are you there?" Gabby's voice quavered.

"I'm coming. I was just trying to see what Clem found, but I can't see anything, it's too dark." I brushed the dirt and dead leaves off my knees and walked quickly back to the main trail. "I think we should head back now. I never thought to bring a flashlight."

"I'm ready whenever you are." Her relief was evident.

I took a last look around to memorize the spot and noticed a tiny bay to our left, a spot in the lake that was almost completely landlocked with just a small opening where the water lapped in and out. That must be where Allison's body was found. It certainly didn't look like a good place to commit suicide, and the trail was flat and clear of roots and branches. There didn't appear to be anything to cause her to fall into the lake. The accident theory didn't hold a lot of water, if you'll pardon the pun. I stuck my hand in my jacket pocket and fingered the matchbook cover. Of course it could have been thrown there by anyone, but it might provide a clue. There must have been someone with Allison that night. There was no way she would have come here alone.

We hurried back to the car, using the fast fading light to guide our way. Gabby was right, it was spooky, but there was no way I was going to admit I felt just as uneasy as she did.

Chapter Eleven

I didn't bother to tell anyone about the matchbook. No reason to get them all upset. When we got home I went to bed almost immediately and left it in my jacket pocket until the next morning when I got to the office. Bill wasn't around, which was just as well. I don't know which of them, Gabby or Bill, worries more about my safety and well-being. That's why I've found it advantageous to keep certain things to myself.

Waterworks Café—the name rang a bell. I had read an article in *Monday Magazine* recently about old buildings near the harbor being renovated and utilized for trendy shops and restaurants. I turned the matches over and read the address on the back. 1455 Third Street. I got out a street map of Victoria and looked it up. It wasn't near the harbor at all. In fact, it was not far from the warehouse where I'd seen Glen Peters and his buddies unloading the truck.

I made one of those executive decisions I'm famous for, deciding not to bother with coffee at the office. I felt like going out, in fact, I felt a lot like trying the Waterworks Café. Did I bother to leave a note for Bill? What do you think? Grabbing the map, I hustled home and picked up the van, hollering through the front door to let Gabby know I had an errand to do and might be late for lunch. I didn't stop to talk. She might ask questions, ones I didn't want to answer. How dangerous could it be to drink a cup of coffee, after all?

Following the map, I drove straight to the café and parked outside. I didn't bother to try to hide the van or myself; after all, I was a legitimate customer. The neighborhood was still as seedy and run-down as it had been a few days before, and the café from the outside blended nicely with the surrounding grunge but the inside looked clean enough. Most of the customers were men in work clothes. The air was thick with smoke and machine oil and I cut my way through it to the only empty table, which was near the kitchen. A tired-looking waitress of uncertain age filled a cup with coffee and brought it to my table automatically, as though it was the only beverage on tap. She handed me a greasy-looking paper menu, with prices crossed out in pencil and new ones written above. I was tempted but told her coffee was fine. I didn't want to add the risk of food poisoning to the other dangers I might be facing. Actually, on second thought, poisoning was probably the least of my worries. From the looks being cast in my direction, I was beginning to regret not having told anyone where I would be. I could disappear off the face of the earth and no one would even know where to start looking.

Once I had taken a couple of sips of coffee to settle my nerves, I looked around nonchalantly at my fellow customers. Nothing out of the ordinary here, just a bunch of guys drinking their coffee, smoking and leering. Did I say *most* of the customers were men? I take that back. I was the only woman, and they were all looking at me as though I was either an extraterrestrial or their next meal. All of a sudden I found my coffee cup extraordinarily fascinating. I studied it intently, not daring to look up in case I caught someone's eye and they mistook my glance for interest. The bell above the door jangled, indicating someone was either entering or leaving, and I chanced a quick look. Two guys were on their way out. Just before they closed the door behind them, they glanced in my direction. My heart leaped into my throat. I've read that phrase in many a thriller, but until that very moment, never believed it possible. I closed my mouth quickly so it didn't jump right out. Glen Peters and the ape truck driver were leaving the café. I hadn't even noticed them, being too preoccupied with my own precarious situation. Had they recognized me? I sure hoped not.

I sat there dumbly sipping my coffee and wondering if I'd chosen the wrong career. All of a sudden, the investigations field was too nerves-wracking for my tastes. I mentally kicked myself around the block for not spotting Peters and his pal and for letting them see me. Just the kind of mistake a rank amateur would make. After a few more minutes of mental gymnastics, I realized I had the info I'd been looking for. If Allison wasn't alone at the Lake, maybe Peters had been with her.

I paid for my coffee and scuttled to the door, a dozen pair of eyes following my every move. When I made to climb into the van, I noticed one of the tires was awfully low, in fact, it was lower than a snake's belly. Flat. Thank goodness I had the cell phone with me—I didn't have to go back into the café to call for help. I had auto club coverage, so I quickly called for someone to come and change the tire. I waited in the van until they showed up. It was a half hour or so before a tow truck appeared. The whole time I felt like a sitting duck, but even though I got a stiff neck from looking over my shoulder, there was no sign of Peters or Tarzan.

The young fellow from the auto club changed the tire in a matter of minutes and I gave him a tip for his trouble. As he was loading the flat tire into the back of the van, something he said sent a shiver dancing down my spine.

"Ma'am, I don't know if you noticed, but this tire has been slashed. Look here." He pointed to a rather large slit in the side of the tire.

My heart sank. Not only did I hate being called ma'am, but I could only think of one person who might have wanted to give me a little warning. Peters. He was telling me he didn't like my snooping. Had the insurance company told him his claim had been denied, or was he upset because I was investigating Allison's death? Either way, he wasn't the sort of person I wanted to tangle with, especially since he traveled in such bad company.

It was time I talked to Trevor again, to find out what he and his partner Fraser knew about Peters. I had asked him to let me know if he could see any connection between Peters and Allison's death. He hadn't called. I'd call *him* as soon as I got back to the office.

Bill was on the phone when I walked into the office.

"Oh, just a minute, here she is now." He turned to me. "It's for you, Sam, someone named Melissa. Says it's really important that she talk to you right away."

"That's Allison's friend. Put it through to my office, will you." I sprinted for my desk and picked up the phone on the first ring.

"Hello, Melissa."

"Sam, we need to talk. Can you pick me up after school?"

"Sure, what's up?"

"I don't have time right now, there goes the bell. I have to be back in class. Just come to the front of the school at three-thirty like last time, okay?"

The phone went dead so rather than stand there like a dummy, I hung up and went back out to where Bill was waiting.

"What did she want?" he asked.

"She didn't say. Just asked me to meet her after school. It sounded important, but you know kids, maybe she chipped her nail polish or something," I joked. "This investigation has more twists and turns than the West Coast Trail."

"Maybe you should fill me in on some of them, Sam. I don't want you getting into trouble."

"Moi? Are you kidding?"

"Sam, what have you been up to?"

"Not much, Mr. Henry. And you can be sure if I need your help, I'll ask for it."

"Since when? You know darn well you never ask for help until it's too late."

"Well, this time I promise I'll tell all, but not yet. All I have right now are a bunch of disconnected bits of information. Wait until I do a bit more sleuthing, then we'll talk."

"I don't know if I trust you. At least promise you'll take the cell phone with you, so you can call for help if things get hot."

"Yes sir." I saluted, and I think he took it the wrong way because he turned on his heel and left, slamming the door behind him. He was always so bossy, always wanting to take over just when things got interesting. Well, I'd tell him all about the case, but not until I was good and ready.

Trevor wasn't in when I called. I left messages at the station and at his home. I knew he'd get back to me when he got one or the other of them. Glancing at my watch I saw it was way past lunchtime, so I headed home.

Melissa was waiting for me outside the school. She hadn't spotted me yet so I had a chance to observe her. She was in a heated conversation with none other than Rob. As I pulled up, he turned and walked away and she scowled at his retreating back. And I had thought they were friends!

"Hi Melissa, hop in," I said, as she opened the door.

"Yeah." She threw her backpack on the floor and climbed into the passenger seat. "Let's get out of here."

"What's up with you and Rob? I thought you were buddies. You seem pretty steamed."

"Men are such jerks. All that macho stuff. I don't want to talk about it. I've got more important things on my mind."

"Like what?"

"Can we go back to that café we went to last time, you know, the one with the jukebox?"

"Sure, no problem. But I thought something was up? On the phone you sounded like you had something urgent to talk to me about."

"I do, but I'll wait until we're at the café." She gave me one of those looks like, "honestly, don't you know anything?" So I shut up and drove.

Fifteen minutes later, we were sipping our shakes, hers chocolate and mine vanilla, and waiting for Lil to bring our smiling cheeseburgers and fries. Melissa still hadn't told me why she'd dragged me out.

"Melissa, remember, you had something important you wanted to discuss," I reminded her. I didn't want to scare her off, but the suspense was killing me.

"I know, I know," she said impatiently. "I was just trying to figure out what to do."

"Maybe I can help?"

"Yeah, you're right. Well, it's like this. I got a call from Mrs. Peters last night. She asked me to baby-sit this weekend. I'm not sure if I should go. I told her I'd call tonight and let her know. What do you think?"

"I don't think it's a good idea. It could be dangerous. Peters may have been the last person to see Allison alive. That makes him suspect in my book."

"That's just it. I've been asking around school and no one seems to have any idea what happened to Allison. They all seem to accept the police finding of suicide or an accident. Case closed, life goes on. Well, it doesn't work for me. Allison was my best friend, and I want to know what happened to her." She stopped talking when Lil brought our burgers to the table, then she looked at me, her eyes wide and watery. "I can't just let them close the books on her death without trying to find out exactly what went down. Have you got a better idea?"

"I'm sure we'll get to the bottom of it, but it takes time," I said weakly.

She wasn't impressed. "Well, if I agree to baby-sit for the Peterses, I might be able to find out something. There's something fishy going on. Allison kind of let a few hints drop, but I was too dumb to pick up on them."

"What kind of hints? What did she say?"

"Nothing definite," Melissa answered hastily. "She mentioned she was thinking of telling Peters she couldn't baby-sit anymore. She said he gave her the creeps. But she was reluctant to give up the job, because it was a steady source of income for her. Her dad wouldn't give her an allowance."

"What did she need the money for?"

"Just hanging out, movies, clothes, you know."

"Well, I vote no, if my opinion matters. I think it's too risky."

"I'm going to do it no matter what you say, Sam,"

she said defiantly, her chin stuck out a mile. "I've made up my mind. Can I call you for help if I need it? I *was* going to ask Rob, but he's acting like such a jerk, I don't want to."

She pleaded and I knew she'd go ahead regardless of what I said, so against my better judgement, I agreed to help her. I made her promise to let me know which nights she was baby-sitting and to call me from the Peters place at least once during the evening and when she got home. I told her I'd carry the cell phone with me at all times. It was the best I could do. I didn't have enough evidence against Peters to go running to the police. I didn't have anything definite at all. Just a feeling, and in my book that wasn't enough. It may have been enough for Gabby, intuition and all, but not for me. I *did* wonder if Melissa knew more than she was willing to admit. Allison had been her best friend after all. They probably told each other everything. And Rob, what about him? Would Allison have confided in him if there was something strange going on at the Peters' house? Perhaps. But neither of them was willing to tell me. I was on the other side of that invisible but indelible line between teens and adults. I'd just have to keep on digging and hope I'd get the dirt I needed to lay Allison to rest.

Chapter Twelve

At home it was the night the Psychic Circle met. I did my disappearing act as usual, and Gabby and her cohorts met until late, burning candles and reciting incantations before and after meditating. When Gabby came upstairs later, I asked politely how things had gone, and she just said, "fine," offering no details. She seemed preoccupied and unusually quiet. I had a lot of things on my mind, too.

The next morning started off well, that is, until Gabby went out to the van to look for a piece of equipment she'd misplaced. She came storming back into the house, and hollered up to me.

"Sam, can you come down here?" I should have picked up on something from the tone of her voice, but I was still preoccupied, worrying about Melissa and her crazy plan of baby-sitting for the Peters, so

I didn't realize just how upset she was until I went downstairs and saw her face, which started out red and blustery, then got very white and still.

"What's up?"

"What the heck happened to that tire in the back of the van?"

"I had a flat yesterday. I have to take it in for repair." I stalled for time. She must have noticed it had been slashed.

"And just how did it happen to go flat?" she demanded, not giving an inch.

"Well, actually it didn't just happen to go flat, someone helped it along. I was parked in a rough area of town yesterday and when I came back out to the van, the tire was flat."

"And of course you have no idea who did it?" she added sarcastically.

"I'm not sure."

"Oh, come on, Sam, you must have an idea."

"I do have an idea, but I wouldn't like to accuse anyone without proof positive," I tried to joke, but my attempt didn't satisfy Gabby.

"And what, may I ask, were you doing in this so-called rough area of town? I thought you promised to tell Bill and me everything, so we wouldn't have to worry."

"I was planning to . . . I just haven't had a chance. Yesterday when I got home, you were getting ready to meet with the Psychic Circle and then you were so quiet last night . . ."

"This is the last straw."

She turned and walked out of the kitchen and I

heard her going upstairs. Clem followed, looking glum. It was suspiciously quiet for ages. Then the phone rang. Gabby must have picked it up right away, as it didn't ring a second time. There was a long silence, then I could hear her moving things around, opening and closing drawers and dragging something heavy. I couldn't figure out what she was up to. That is, until she came downstairs, lugging a large suitcase.

"What are you doing, Gab? I'm sorry, I know I should have told you about the tire. I just never thought—"

"That's the story of your life. You never think. Anyway, I can't worry about that right now; something has come up. My mom has had a slight heart attack and is in the hospital. I told my father I would come and look after the house for him for a few days. Will you drive me to the ferry terminal? If we leave right now, I should be able to get the eleven o'clock ferry. And I'm taking Clem with me."

"Oh, Gabby, I'm sorry, I hope your mom will be okay."

Tears welled up in Gabby's eyes and she gave me a frightened look.

"Sam, I'm scared. I hope she's all right. And I'm worried about you, too. I wish I didn't have to go away right now, but I do."

"Don't worry about me, I'll manage fine, and I've got Bill to look after me while you're away. He won't let me get away with anything," I joked feebly.

She sat silently next to me all the way to the ferry terminal. As soon as I stopped the van, she and Clem got out, and she turned to me, "I'll be in touch. Take care of yourself, Sam."

She didn't look back as Mimi and I sat glumly watching her and Clem walk to the terminal and go inside. The automatic doors closed behind them and they disappeared out of sight. I sat there a few moments longer, then started the van and drove back toward town. Gabby and I were like family. And I knew her parents well, so I was also worried about her mother.

I didn't much like the idea of returning to the apartment alone. Mimi and I drove around a little, then I parked the van near the water and watched the waves lap on the shore. Eventually, I had no choice but to take Mimi home. She had already begun to miss Clem. When we arrived at the apartment, she ran quickly to the door and then from room to room, looking for her. When she couldn't find her, she lay down on her mat in the kitchen and gave me a sorrowful look, as if asking what had I done to make them go away.

It hadn't seemed like such a serious transgression to omit telling Gabby about the tire. She was overreacting, I thought. Then I realized it didn't really matter what I thought. And truthfully, I knew she was not really angry, only worried about my safety.

I couldn't stand the apartment, so after lunch Mimi and I walked to the office. I would try to salvage the day by putting in some work on the book and perhaps trying again to get hold of Trevor. I really wanted to talk to him about Peters, especially in light of Melissa's plan.

* * *

The light on the answering machine was blinking urgently when I unlocked the office door. Bill was nowhere to be seen. I punched the button. It was Melissa. She said she'd called the Peterses and told them she was free to baby-sit that night. She said she'd call after they went out and Tommy was in bed. She added, "Don't worry, Sam. I can look after myself." In some strange way, her behavior toward me reminded me of mine toward Gabby. No wonder Gabby got upset. But all my life I had been famous for rushing headlong into every imaginable kind of trouble. I didn't know if an old dog like me could learn new tricks.

"What do you think, Mimi? Is it too late for me?"

Mimi looked up at me mournfully. She and Clem were inseparable. She didn't understand where her friend had gone.

Thank goodness Bill chose that precise moment to show up at the office, to interrupt our wallowing in misery. He was all smiles.

"Sam, we hardly ever see each other. How are things?"

"Peachy keen, Bill, just wonderful."

"Uh-oh, do I detect a note of sarcasm? Come and tell Billy all about it." He patted the couch beside him and I obediently sat down.

"Seriously, what's the matter, Sam? You seem pretty glum."

"Gabby's mother is in the hospital. She left this morning to go and help her family, and she took Clem with her. And she was a little upset with me, too. We didn't have a chance to patch up our misunderstanding."

"Hmm. What did you do? Did she find out about your meat eating?" he joked.

"Just because I neglected to tell her that the tire on the van had been slashed, she got all hot and bothered."

"Wait a minute, back up. What's this about a slashed tire?"

"Not you, too! You'd think someone had tried to slit my throat. It was worn out anyway. I had been planning to buy some new ones this summer."

"Sam, when and where did this happen?" Bill asked sternly.

"Yesterday, down near the Waterworks Café."

"What were you doing down there? That's not exactly the best neighborhood."

"I was out at Elk Lake a couple of days ago and I happened to find a matchbook cover on the ground, underneath some bushes. I owe that to Clem, she was digging—"

"Never mind Clem," he interrupted. "Are you talking about the site where Allison's body was found?"

"Yeah. Gabby and I took a little walk with the dogs a couple of nights ago. I found the matchbook cover in the general area where she was found and I was thinking perhaps someone who was with her might have dropped it there. The matches were from the Waterworks Café. I went there for coffee because I wanted to see what kind of a place it was. You'll never guess who was there."

"Honestly, Sam, no wonder Gabby gets worried. Don't you have any common sense? I'm beginning to wonder if it was such a good idea to get you involved in this business. You're just not trained to go running around after possible murderers. Who did you see?"

I was mad enough at him that I almost didn't answer, but then I thought that's what got me into trouble with Gabby. I'd better tell all. "Glen Peters and his henchman, the truck driver I mentioned in the insurance report, were in the café. Just after I got there, they left. When I went outside the tire had been slashed. I don't know if Glen's mad because his insurance claim was denied and he's somehow connected me with it. Or is his problem that he had something to do with Allison's death and he was spooked by me coming to his house to talk to him and his wife? Or was he just mad about seeing me at his favorite watering hole? Take your pick."

"I think it's time we worked on this file together. Your family, not to mention Gabby and Emily, will kill me if anything happens to you. Now, what do you say, are you ready to let me help?"

"Well, I *am* a little concerned about the way things are going. First there's Trevor and the drug investigation, then there's Melissa and her scheme to babysit for Peters—"

"Wait a minute, back up. What did you say about Trevor?"

It took me the rest of the afternoon to fill Bill in on Melissa and Rob, and Trevor's involvement. We agreed I would continue to follow up on any leads and report back each evening. Together we would decide on what action, if any, should be taken. Even though I wouldn't admit it, I was secretly relieved not to have all the responsibility for the investigation. I took the cell phone and went home, picking up a barbecued chicken and salads from the local deli for supper.

Mimi and I curled up in front of the television waiting for Melissa's call. It came around ten. She had nothing out of the ordinary to report and agreed to call again when she got home. I dozed in front of the TV until she called again at midnight to say she had arrived home safely, then went to bed.

Chapter Thirteen

I finally caught up with Trevor the next morning. He apologized for not getting back to me sooner.

"Never mind, Trevor. I'm just glad it wasn't a dire emergency. Where the heck are Victoria's finest when you need them? Out giving people photo radar tickets, I guess."

"What's up, Sam? This is supposed to be my day off."

"Were you able to talk to the investigating officers on the Allison Gillespie case? I'm anxious to know if they were interested that one of the last people who saw her alive was Glen Peters, a man involved in the local drug scene."

"I talked to them, but they don't feel there's any connection. And I can't really see one myself. I think it's just coincidence that Allison happened to be babysitting for the Peterses. The autopsy done on the girl didn't pick up any drugs in her system—just a small amount of alcohol. And there's nothing to link Peters to the spot where her body was found. The investigating officers still feel their conclusion is the right one. They think she died accidentally or by suicide."

"What about your drug investigation? How's that going?"

"The day we saw you was only the second time we'd staked out the house. It's very preliminary at this stage."

"Okay, if you don't have anything further, I'll let you get back to your day off. *I've* got lots of work to do. Don't forget to call if you find out anything about Allison."

"Will do."

"Oh and Trevor, say hi to Fraser for me, will you?"

The weekend stretched in front of me like an empty page. I had the same feeling as when I was trying to write and the words wouldn't come. I had no idea what I was going to do to fill the time. Melissa had told me she wasn't going to be baby-sitting again for the Peters kid until the following Tuesday. It looked as though Mimi and I would have to find a way to amuse ourselves.

I thought about Martha and about my father. I wondered if they had made plans for the weekend. I decided to get on the blower and see what I could set up.

Richard had no plans, at least none he considered more important than meeting his older daughter. He would come to Victoria the next day, if Martha was available. Crossing my fingers, I called her. She was home.

"Martha, it's me."

"Hello me."

"I've invited Richard over tomorrow. Can you be at my place around two?"

"I thought you were going to give me time to think this over."

"You've had all week. Come on, Martha, it's just like when we would go swimming in the ocean as kids. You always needed to be pushed. Once you were in, the water was fine."

"I fail to see the similarity," she bristled. "Besides, I haven't even had a chance to talk to Hugo, or Mother."

"You've got today. I've got it all set up for tomorrow at two. I hope you'll be there. Gotta run." I hung up quickly before she could come up with any more excuses.

Dad arrived at the apartment about one-thirty, just as I was starting a pot of coffee and setting out a plate of store-bought cookies. He looked as nervous as I felt.

"Sam, it's good to see you," he said as I gave him a hug. "Where's Gabby?"

"She had to make an unexpected trip to Vancouver. Her mother's not well."

"I hope everything's okay."

"I'm sure it will be."

"Your sister's not here yet?" Richard asked, looking around nervously.

"Don't worry, she'll be here. She's always late. I swear that girl will be late for her own funeral," I joked, and then realized from the look on his face, that it wasn't from him I had inherited my zany sense of humor. My only excuse is that I still had Allison's funeral on the brain—in fact, the whole situation was bugging the heck out of me.

The doorbell sounded and I jumped up eagerly. "You stay here, I'll go and let Martha in," I said, thinking to give Richard time to compose himself. I glanced at my watch and noticed it still wasn't two o'clock. If that was Martha, it would be the first time she'd arrived early since the day she was born.

"Melissa." I stepped back, surprised to see her standing on the porch.

"Sam, I hope it's okay to come over without calling, but I needed to talk to you right away and I didn't want to take a chance that my parents would overhear me. Sam, I'm scared!"

She burst into tears, and when I stepped forward to comfort her, noticed she had looked up in alarm. She had just noticed Richard who had come up behind me.

"Martha? No, it can't be, this child is much too young. Sam?" There was confusion in his voice.

"Dad, this is Melissa. She's a friend. I'm just going to take her upstairs to my office and I'll be right back. Can you keep a lookout for Martha?"

He looked as if he were going to bolt and run. He had been counting on me to act as a buffer during their first meeting, but it couldn't be helped.

I hustled Melissa up the stairs, explaining briefly on the way, that I would have to leave her by herself temporarily while I took care of business downstairs, but I would be back as soon as I could to discuss whatever was bothering her. I zipped down to the kitchen to grab a Coke and some snack foods to keep her busy, running them back up. I no sooner arrived upstairs when I heard the doorbell again. Tossing the Coke to Melissa, I asked her to make herself at home and I'd be back ASAP.

In my haste I practically fell down the stairs, sliding down the last two or three to land in a heap at the bottom.

"Sam, are you all right? What's going on?" She looked puzzled.

"Just dandy!" I was huffing and puffing from my two quick trips up and down the stairs, and I paused to get my breath.

Martha stepped inside the apartment and put down the baby carrier she had been holding. Timothy was sound asleep and looking like an angel. She glanced around nervously. It did my heart good to see Martha—calm, cool Martha—unmasked.

"He's in the living room. You go on in while I take off Tim's jacket and get him comfortable."

"Come with me," she whispered. "I can't do this alone."

"Don't worry," I said. "Dad is just as nervous as you. He won't bite."

"Sam, please," she begged urgently.

"Oh, all right. Let's go." I called out as I picked up the baby, carrier and all, "Dad, Martha and Timothy are here."

He was standing just inside the living room, his

hand on Mimi's head for support. She was trying to lick his hand, oblivious to the tension in the room.

"Martha, I've hoped and prayed for this moment." He wiped away a tear with the back of his hand.

"Dad, I don't know what to say, it's been so long. I wouldn't have known you."

They both stood still eyeing each other like a couple of strange dogs. Just then Tim saved the day. He had woken and looked around and not seeing his mother, started fussing.

Martha bent over and scooped him up out of the seat. She walked toward Dad hesitantly. "This is your grandson, Timothy."

"He's beautiful. I can see a little of you in his face, but I'll bet he looks a lot like his father."

"You're right."

"May I hold him?"

"Of course, why don't you sit down on the sofa?"

"Good idea, my legs feel like jelly." He laughed ruefully.

"I'll sit next to you. Otherwise he might start to cry."

"If anybody cares, I'll go and get some coffee," I said, feeling like a fifth wheel.

"What?" Martha asked. "Oh, sure Sam, do that."

I went to the kitchen and put the coffee carafe on a tray with the cream and sugar and the plate of cookies, and brought them into the living room.

"I think I'll just leave the three of you to get acquainted, while I go and tend to my other guest."

"Okay, Sam," Martha said, not even thinking to ask

what other guest I could possibly have at a time like this.

I was feeling a little miffed, but at the same time relieved that the meeting had finally taken place. Next time, and I was sure there would be a next time, it would be easier.

Melissa was sitting at my desk, playing on the computer when I got back upstairs to the office.

"I hope you don't mind, Sam. I didn't know what to do. I just turned it on and found the games. Everyone has games," she offered by way of explanation.

"As long as you didn't wipe out my manuscript. I sweat blood over every word. I'd be inclined to kill anyone who messed with it," I said, not even thinking about what I'd said until I saw her horror-struck expression.

"I'm sorry, Melissa, that was thoughtless of me. Now why don't you tell me what's happened? You seemed upset when you got here."

"I feel better now. Maybe I was just imagining things. Maybe everything's okay," she said distractedly, still looking at the computer screen and her game of solitaire.

"Melissa, something got you upset enough that you came rushing over here without even calling. What was it?" I asked impatiently.

"Actually, it's a couple of things. First there's Rob. He's acting real strange. He called me yesterday and was asking me about Mr. Peters. He wanted to know if I'd seen anything strange going on at their house. He said Allison had told him something. He wouldn't tell me what it was. He wanted me to tell him everything about the place, to see if I had noticed the same things. Then he said something crazy. Something like, 'I'm going to call that dude and tell him I know what Allison knew. I figure she must have known something and that's what got her into trouble.' "

"How does he know Allison was in trouble?"

"That's what I asked him, but he wouldn't say."

"Do you think he really knows something about Peters or is he just bluffing?"

"Man, I don't know. I think he's bluffing, but I'm not sure. What if he does know something? Doesn't that mean he could be in danger? I mean, we don't know if Allison was murdered, but if she was, you know, wouldn't that mean that Rob might be making himself a target, too?"

"You're right. Darn. I had a good talk with Rob the other day and he said he didn't have any idea what could have happened to Allison. What's he trying to pull?"

"I don't know."

"Melissa, you said there were a couple of things. What was the other one?"

"Oh, yeah. Well, the other night when I was at Mr. and Mrs. Peters's place, I heard them arguing just before they went out. I was in Tommy's bedroom and they were getting ready to go, in their bedroom next door. I heard her say to him, 'Do you think it's a good idea to have Melissa here? Look what happened to Allison,' and he said, 'Quit worrying, will ya? I told Jim to make sure that the guys don't bring any stuff to the house when we're not home. He screwed up last time, but it won't happen again.' Then they went out and I got busy with Tommy and forgot about what he said until today when Rob called."

"Did you tell Rob about this?" I asked urgently.

"No way, man. I'm afraid to tell him anything. I think he's gone a little crazy. What should we do?"

Should I tell her about Trevor and Fraser and their suspicions about Peters being into the drug trade? No, the less she knew the better.

"I think you should stay away from the Peters place. Don't go baby-sitting there anymore until we get to the bottom of this. I don't want anything to happen to you. Maybe he's not involved at all, but we can't take any chances."

"Maybe you're right, but then how are we going to find out what happened to Allison?"

"Why don't you leave that to me?"

"I want to help. She was *my* friend."

"I know, Melissa, but the best thing you can do is to keep your eyes and ears open at school and let me know if you hear anything more. Keep an eye on Rob, and let me know if he gets up to anything strange, okay?"

"Oh, all right," she agreed reluctantly.

"Now, let me drive you home."

"I've got my mom's car, I have my license now," she said proudly.

"Okay, I'll see you to the door, then. Promise to keep in touch. Why don't you call me every night around eleven o'clock? Just to report in. And I'll let you know what I find out, too."

"Kind of like partners?" she asked, her eyes lighting up.

"Yeah, just like partners." Just what I needed, another partner.

"Thanks, Sam." She ran lightly down the steps and to her mother's car. "I'll call tomorrow night."

" 'Bye, Melissa. Drive carefully."

She gave me one of those looks and slammed the car door, starting the engine with a roar and backing out of the driveway, barely missing Jill's car, which was parked on the street in front of the house.

Back inside, I heard the sound of low voices coming from the living room as I tried to creep past the open door without being seen.

"Sam, come in here." It was Martha, and she was using her "don't mess with me" voice.

"How are things going, Martha, Dad? Everything okay?"

"Sam." Martha got up and gave me a big hug. "Thanks for insisting that I meet with Dad. It's been wonderful." She was beaming and so was he, as he bounced his grandson on his knee. "I'm just going to take Dad over to meet Stephen and have a bite to eat. Do you want to come along? Dad says Gabby's away."

"Yes, she had to go to help her parents. Thanks for the invite, but I think I'll stay here. I'm bushed. It's been a busy day and I still have a lot to do," I fibbed. I didn't want to rain on their parade.

I was in a filthy mood, one which would be better handled by holing up in my study with a large chocolate bar and a carton of ice cream. I know—there's no accounting for some people's taste. I hurried them out the door, promising to call them both, and yes, we'd all get together for dinner soon.

I put on my fuzziest PJs and curled up in front of the television with Mimi sitting forlornly on my feet, jumping up at the slightest sound and running to the door. The chocolate was good and the ice cream lifted my spirits. I eventually drifted off to sleep and woke up to the high-pitched drone of a television station that has gone off the air. I got up wearily and went to bed.

Chapter Fourteen

After my chat with Melissa the night before, I awoke with a feeling of dread in the pit of my stomach. What was I going to do about Rob? I was afraid that little punk would do something stupid and get himself killed like Allison.

And when had I started thinking of Allison's death as murder? I can't say precisely, but I felt absolutely certain. The only problem was, I had no idea of who had done it or why. Well, I had an idea of who, but couldn't prove anything. For that matter, I even had an idea of why. But it seemed strange to me that Trevor and Fraser and the rest of Victoria's finest had not been able to put two and two together. So was I totally out to lunch? Or did I just happen to be in possession of a couple of small pieces of information that the others didn't have? The police who had investigated Allison's death hadn't known about Peters's drug connections or that Allison was his baby-sitter. The drug squad had not known about Allison's death, until I pointed it out. Neither of them knew I had been to the scene of her death and found a match cover that possibly implicated Peters.

And what did Rob know? Had he learned something from Allison before her death, something that could tie all the facts together? Melissa didn't seem to know. The only thing to do was to call on Rob again and bully the information out of him. I would stop by the school around three and try and catch him as he left for home. I wanted to talk to him away from the watchful eyes of his mother.

Gabby still hadn't called. The day was as dark and gloomy as I felt. I had a scalding shower and dressed warmly, gulped down a coffee, and headed to the office, Mimi in tow. She was off her food. I had made her a nice bowl of scrambled eggs but she just sniffed at them and walked away, lying down beside my chair. I was more worried about her than myself.

Bill was whistling in the office as I trudged up the stairs. He greeted me with a smile and a "How are you?" Then he looked at my face and fell silent. Within a few minutes the traitor thought of some urgent business he had to conduct downtown and left Mimi and I to our misery.

The day dragged on and on, but finally it was nearing two-thirty, so Mimi and I walked home to pick up the van and left for Saanich and the secondary school. I pulled up in the same spot I had picked up Melissa before, and kept a look out for Rob. At about three-thirty he finally emerged, alone and looking almost as down as us.

"Rob, over here," I called. He looked up, startled, and then recognized me and sauntered over to the van.

"Ms. Hope, what are you doing here? Are you looking for Melissa?"

"Call me Sam, please, you make me feel a hundred years old. And, no, I'm not here to see Melissa—I was looking for you. Hop in and I'll give you a lift home."

"Sure." He opened the door and eyed Mimi who was stretched out on the seat. She hardly even bothered to look up at him.

"What's wrong with your dog? She looks sick," he said.

"She's got a broken heart. Her friend has gone away. Mimi, get down, in the back." I pulled at her collar, and she climbed down and lay on the floor in the back of the van. "Jump in, just brush off the dog hair," I said.

"Don't worry about it. I like dogs." He smiled. "She's a beauty." He looked puzzled. "So what's up, Sam? I thought we'd covered everything the other day. Have you found out something new?"

"I was hoping *you* might know something, Rob. Melissa said you mentioned something to her. That Allison told you something about the Peters place before she disappeared."

"What a blabbermouth that girl is! I just asked her if she had noticed anything strange. I've been going over and over things in my mind. I don't think Allison committed suicide. And an accident way out at Elk

Lake doesn't make much sense. And where was she before she disappeared? At the Peters place, looking after that kid of theirs. They were the last people to see her alive. At least that's what I think."

"I'm with you so far. That's the conclusion I've reached myself. But what did Allison say that prompted you to ask Melissa if she had noticed anything unusual?"

"It wasn't just before she disappeared, okay, it was a couple of weeks before. She had been baby-sitting and called me to pick her up. I went there and waited outside for her. When she came out, she practically ran to the car, jumped in, and locked the door. She told me to get going and wouldn't say anything more until we were miles away. Then she made me pull over and threw herself into my arms. I would have been delighted, except that she was shaking all over. She wouldn't tell me what was wrong. I kept bugging her and finally she said something like, if Glen finds out I saw what his buddies put in the garage, he'll kill me. Honestly, Sam, I thought she was just being hysterical. I didn't think she was in any danger. She wouldn't tell me what she saw. After a while she calmed down and I took her home. She didn't mention it again, and then a few days later, we had the fight I told you about and then she disappeared. At first, like I told you, I thought maybe she'd killed herself because of our fight. Then I started going back in my mind over all the things she'd said and done just before she went missing. When I remembered what she'd said about Peters, I called Melissa to find out if she knew anything. Those two usually told each other everything. But she had no idea what I was talking about. That's when I really started to worry. Allison must have been seriously scared, or she would have discussed this with Melissa, or even with me again. But she never mentioned the subject again." He sat back glumly. "If I had taken her seriously, she might still be alive today."

"Hey, hold on. We don't know if Peters was involved, you're jumping to some pretty major conclusions. You know, what I'd like to know is how did Allison start baby-sitting for the Peterses? Was it Melissa who got her the job?"

"I don't think so. No, I remember Allison telling me her dad had told her he wasn't going to give her an allowance any more. He said she should earn her own spending money. He said he knew someone who was looking for a baby-sitter and she should give the people a call. That's how she got Mrs. Peters's name and phone number. I wondered at the time how Mr. Gillespie would know a guy like Peters. I mean, they're not in the same league at all. You've met Allison's old man, haven't you?"

I nodded.

"Then you know what I mean."

"Allison didn't tell you how her father and Peters had met."

"No, I don't think she knew. She and her dad didn't talk much. He was so strict, and besides, he was hardly ever home. He was always travelling out of the country."

"Where did he go?"

"I don't know. All over the place I think. Sometimes he went to the States or South America or even Hong Kong. Allison had a few souvenirs from different places. He never told her or her mother what he was doing. He just said he had to go away on business. I don't think Allison even knew what kind of work he did. Strange, don't you think?"

"Let's not let our imaginations run away with us, Rob. I'm sure Allison's father is a perfectly respectable businessman. Even if he is a real jerk."

"You can say that again," he agreed. "So what are we going to do, Sam? See, what I was thinking was this. I was thinking about calling Peters and telling him that Allison saw what he had hidden in his garage, and she told me about it. I was going to tell him I wanted a piece of the action or I'd go to the police. What do you think?" he looked at me earnestly, and suddenly I realized just how young he was.

"Rob, this isn't like some cops and robbers show on TV. Allison is dead. We don't know how she got that way. We can't afford to take any chances. I agree we should use this information to try to find out if Peters is involved, but I need to talk to my partner and some of his cop buddies, and see if they can think of a way to do this without putting you in danger."

"I'll wait a couple of days, but if you don't come up with something, I'm going to try it my way," Rob insisted. "I want to know what happened to Allison." His voice had a tone of finality in it, and I could feel that knot in my stomach swell and grow until it threatened to reach up and choke me.

I dropped Rob off, extracting a promise from him that he wouldn't contact Peters without talking to me first. I had given him my cell phone number and told him, as I had done with Melissa, to call anytime, if he felt himself in danger. I made tracks for home.

I was getting really worried about Mimi. She hadn't eaten a proper meal since Clem and Gabby had left. When we got home, she followed me into the house and lay down on her mat in the kitchen. I coaxed her with all her favorite treats—a piece of cheese, a carrot, and even an oatmeal cookie, any and all of which would normally have been eagerly accepted. She turned her face away and rested her head glumly on her paws. If this kept up I'd have to take her to the vet and see if there was something they could do to stimulate her appetite.

From home, I called the office to check for messages. Ethel had called, checking in. I wished I had something to report, but thought better of telling her my suspicions. I put off calling her back.

Bill had called and left a message as well. He said he had to make a quick trip to Vancouver the next day and would be back late tomorrow night. He said we should meet the following day at nine in the morning to talk over progress on Allison's file. That worried me a little. I had wanted to share Rob's information with him right away. I was worried the kid would do something rash if I didn't come up with a plan.

I went to bed, but didn't sleep. Tossing and turning, I finally had a brilliant idea in the wee hours and after mulling it over for a while, drifted off to sleep. Consequently, I didn't wake up until almost noon the next day, and when I did, I felt as though I'd been run over by a Mack truck. I was hot and my body ached all over.

Now, I hardly ever get sick, and when I do, I'm not a happy camper. All I want to do is hide under the covers and wait for the bug or me to die a natural death. But I couldn't just stay in bed. I had two loose cannons out there and they needed defusing.

I forced myself to get up and take a hot shower. I pumped myself full of vitamins and coffee and went to the office. There I wrote down my plan, examined it from all angles, picked it apart, just the way Bill would do when he found out, and then put it back together until I thought I had it right.

I checked in with Rob after school, telling him to hang on, that I thought I had found a way to find out if Peters was involved in Allison's death. When pressed for details, I merely said I'd get back to him when they were all worked out. Then I went home, slurped down a bowl of chicken noodle soup, the only thing that really works for colds and fevers, and waited for Melissa to check in. She phoned earlier than her usual eleven.

"Sam, I'm at the Peters place."

"Melissa, what the heck, I thought I told you not to go there anymore," I practically hollered into the phone.

"Hey, it's not easy to say no. They expect me to take Allison's place and before Rob made me nervous, I had already said I would. Anyway, things are pretty quiet. I even sneaked a peak in the garage. I couldn't see anything."

"Melissa." Now I was upset. "For heaven's sake don't do or say anything to make Peters suspicious. And call me as soon as you get home."

"All right, all right. You're not my mother, you know, Sam."

"Darn right I'm not. If I were, you'd be at home in bed. Just call, you hear?"

"I hear." She hung up.

If only Bill were home. Just like a man. Where the heck are they when you need them? I fussed and fumed pacing up and down while I waited to hear back from Melissa. Mimi looked at me from the corner, not even bothering to get up and follow me as was her usual habit. I went downstairs to the kitchen to see if I could find some tidbit she wouldn't be able to resist. The only thing I could come up with was a piece of cooked chicken in the freezer. I nuked it and chopped it into little pieces, placing a few of them in her bowl with some of her crunchy dog food and a bit of grated cheese. It looked better than what I had eaten for dinner, which was nothing.

The odor of the chicken had made me hungry and I quickly made myself a sandwich which I carried upstairs along with Mimi's bowl. She lifted her head as I came into the office.

"Come on, Mimi, come and have some supper. Look, I'm going to have mine," I coaxed.

She sniffed the air and seemed to think about it. I could almost hear her: "Mmm, chicken, well, maybe a few mouthfuls wouldn't hurt." She picked herself up and ambled slowly over to me. My sandwich, on its plate, with a dill pickle beside it, was sitting on a low coffee table. Ignoring the bowl of food I had prepared for her, she came over and sniffed the sandwich and then before I could say anything, picked it up in her teeth and swallowed it whole. I was so glad to see her eat something, that I didn't even scold her. The sandwich whetted her appetite. She went to her bowl and polished off her own food in a few gulps, looking around for more. Sadly, seeing nothing, she took herself downstairs, and I could hear her great lapping noises as she drank noisily from her water bowl. I followed her down and patted her enthusiastically as she shook her head and showered me with water. At least one of us was fed, and about to reenter the land of the living. I let her out for a run and while she was outside, foraged again in the fridge. No cream for coffee, no food other than a stale piece of cheese and a couple of eggs.

"Hey, Mimi, let's hit the Golden Arches. I'm starving," I said, grabbing the keys to the van off the counter and following Mimi out the door.

I vowed to go grocery shopping the next day. Just because I was fending for myself was no excuse to neglect my health. I'd stock up on chicken noodle soup and frozen dinners. I'd prove I could get along just fine on my own.

Chapter Fifteen

I'll admit I was very happy to see Bill the next morning at the office, and so was Mimi. She was getting tired of my company. I was still under the weather, coughing and sneezing and emitting an odor of cough drops and mentholatum, which I had slathered on my chest the night before. Nevertheless, I had the coffee made by the time he came in.

"It's about time. Where the heck were you yesterday? Just when I need you, you take off," I groused.

"You mean Sam the Invincible is admitting she needs my help?" he asked, savoring his victory.

"Don't rub it in, or go getting a big head. Things are hopping in the Gillespie case, and I know how you worry. I didn't want to go ahead and take action without discussing my plans with you."

"You know, Sam, you're almost human this morning, in spite of your germs. Whatever you do, don't touch me. Now what do you have in mind?"

"First I need to tell you about Melissa and Rob." I proceeded to fill him in on events of the past couple of days. "I don't want those kids turning themselves into bait. So I had this idea. What if *I* were to call Peters myself, tell him Allison had left a diary and her parents had given it to me to read, to see if I could turn up some clues as to what happened to her? I could tell him he figured prominently in it, and that I knew about his business and wanted money to keep quiet. I think he'd fall for it, don't you?"

"Are you crazy?" he yelled. "I should have known. Just when I thought you were coming to your senses. What's gotten into you?"

"I just don't want to see that low-life get away with anything. Oh, I know, we don't really know if he's the guilty party, but I have my suspicions. If he had nothing to do with it, he won't know what I'm talking about and no harm done. If he gets pushy or tries to make a deal or set up a meeting, then we'll still have time to talk to Trevor or whoever down at the station, and see if they can help us out. I'm not going to go rushing in there without backup. I'm not crazy, you know."

"You sure do a good imitation. Is this because you've got a death wish or something?"

"Bill, honestly, I'm just trying to get to the bottom of this mess."

"Okay, let's look at the situation realistically. Don't you think Peters would be more likely to react to one of the kids calling him than you? He's not stupid, he's going to know it's a setup if you call. What we need to do is find someone that can pretend to be either Melissa or Rob, and have that person call. That would make more sense."

"Who do we know that can fill in for either of them? I'm too old and don't look anything like Melissa. Rob is much smaller than you. Hmm."

"You know, Sam, from your description of Melissa, she sounds like she has the same build and coloring as Gabby."

"You know what, Bill, you're the crazy one in this partnership. What are you talking about?" I hollered.

The thing is he was right. There was some physical similarity between Gabby and Melissa. Their coloring was close enough that from a distance they could be mistaken for one another.

"I just thought, if you're so sure that this is a good idea, and not dangerous, you wouldn't mind asking Gabby to do this little thing. Call it a favor, in the interest of justice," he said mildly.

Oh, he was so cagey. Not only had he found a way to involve Gabby in the case, but he had also given me an excuse to contact her and ask for her help, which would go a long way to mending our friendship.

"No, I won't hear of it. Besides, there's no way Gabby would even consider doing this. Isn't there some police woman in the downtown office that could double for Melissa?"

"I don't think so. They are all much bigger than Melissa. You said she was quite short."

"She is."

"Well, why don't you give Gabby a chance to consider the idea. All you have to do is call her and explain what you have in mind, and if she says no, we'll find another way to get to Peters."

"I don't know . . ." I said doubtfully. "Let me think about it and I'll tell you what I've decided in the morning."

"Don't wait too long. One of those kids is liable to do something stupid and impulsive."

"You've got that right."

Knowing I wouldn't be able to get any work done, I figured I might as well go home so I grabbed my jacket and Mimi's leash and set off down the stairs and out into the fresh air. The weather had turned mild and many of the gardens on our street already had bulbs up and blooming. There were even some roses budding. I stopped to sniff a particularly beautiful one that grew on a trellis near the sidewalk. Mimi strained at her leash. She wanted me to hurry up. As we approached the house, she started to whine and pull even harder.

"What's wrong, old girl?" I asked. She just kept pulling until she yanked the leash right out of my hand and took off in the direction of the house. She had never run off before so I was puzzled. Was there something wrong at the house? She was a few hundred yards ahead of me now and barking loudly. She tore up the stairs and howled at the door. It opened, and she went inside. What the heck?

Then it dawned on me. There was only one reason Mimi would run off and leave me standing in the street. Clem must be home. My hopes soared. If Clem was home, then Gabby must be, too. I picked up my pace until I was running, too. Not being in the greatest of shape, by the time I reached the gate, opened it and ran up the front stairs, I was huffing and puffing like the big, bad wolf.

I paused to catch my breath before opening the door. As I stood there, I noticed a delectable smell wafting from the house. She was back and she was cooking.

She was standing over the stove stirring a pot, and hardly looked up. Uh-oh, just because she was back, didn't mean she had forgiven me. Was it because I'd left three days dishes in the sink that morning when I left for work? Or was she still ticked off about the slashed tire? Take your pick.

"Gabby, it's so good to see you. How's your mom?"

"She's doing fine. On the road to recovery."

"I'm so glad." I hesitated. "Gab, I'm sorry, I truly am. I should have told you and Bill about the tire, but I didn't want anyone to worry."

"When will you learn, Sam? The only way people won't worry is if they know what's going on. Do you see my point?"

"Yes, the minute you left I knew you were right. I promise I won't pull a stunt like that again. Am I forgiven?"

"Well, I guess so. I missed you, too," she said, with a smile.

"I thought Mimi would expire from loneliness. She missed Clem terribly."

"Fill me in on what's been going on while I've been gone."

We went into the living room and I spent the next hour telling her all about Rob and Melissa and Dad's meeting with Martha. Finally I got to the point in the story when I had to tell her about Bill's idea that she stand in for Melissa in contacting Peters.

"I knew you and Bill needed my help, that's really why I came home, Sam."

"What do you mean?" How could she have known this was going to come up?

"While I was in Vancouver I had my cards read—you know, tarot. The reader said a friend needed me and that I should travel over water to get to her if necessary. She said, a mystery will be solved. I figured it had to have something to do with Allison."

"Oh," I said weakly. Our reunion was going so well, I wasn't going to risk spoiling it by telling her that Tarot business was a bunch of hooey.

"Gabby, this was Bill's idea. I'm not sure I agree. I don't want the kids to approach Peters, but at the same time, I don't want to put you in danger."

"You were prepared to call this Peters guy yourself. If you can do it, why not me? Don't you think I can handle it?"

A great deal hinged on my response so I chose my words carefully.

"I'm not worried about you calling. What I'm worried about is what happens after. Like what if he wants to meet you? If he did kill Allison, then he won't hesitate to kill again, especially if he thinks someone is on to him."

"But didn't you say you would have it all set up with the police? That they would set a trap with me as bait but be there to step in when the time was right?"

"Yes, but—"

"Never mind the *but*, I'm going to do it and that's that. I want to help. I keep thinking about Ethel Beauchamp and about Allison. Ethel deserves to know what happened to her granddaughter."

"Oh, alright. But I want you to promise that if you change your mind, or if for any reason you want out, you'll say so."

"We're going to see this through together Sam. I'll be fine, silly. Bill wouldn't have suggested this if he thought I would be in any danger. You know that."

"You're right. Oh, I'd better call him and let him know. We need to plan just how we're going to pull this off. But first, I'm starved. I haven't had a good meal since you left. I could eat a horse. Oops, I mean I'm so hungry I could eat tofu!"

Chapter Sixteen

The next night we held a war council in the living room. Bill was there along with Trevor and his partner, Fraser, two detectives from homicide and Gabby and I. We went through several pots of coffee while hatching our plot to send Gabby into battle against Peters.

Everyone thought Peters had something to do with Allison's death, though we hadn't worked out exactly what had happened. We figured it must have something to do with the illegal drugs he had hidden in his garage. If she had seen them, he could have discovered that she knew about his operation.

Trevor and Fraser had been watching his house every day since we had had our close encounter. They knew all about his activities at the warehouse. It was the focal point of his drug operation—where the drugs arrived and where they were shipped off to distributors.

Everyone agreed that we had to act quickly to avoid Rob and Melissa taking matters into their own hands. No one, including me, liked the idea of Gabby doubling for Melissa, but so far no one had come up with a better idea. It was decided that Gabby would make a call the next night, try to blackmail Peters and see how he reacted. She'd try to get him to agree to meet her somewhere, preferably at a spot where the others could be hidden close by. Trevor and Fraser, along with the homicide detectives would provide backup.

Bill and I were relegated to sitting at home, waiting to see what happened. I was not the least bit happy about this turn of events, especially since it was my case and I had wanted to do the job myself. But even I had to admit that the plan would be more likely to succeed if I were not directly involved. Peters would smell a rat if I were the one to make the call.

Gabby was a little nervous, but considering that she had never been particularly interested in becoming involved in my snooping, I thought she was handling it quite well. She asked a lot of questions about how she should behave and what she should demand from Peters. It was agreed that she would tell him she wanted to meet him at the warehouse. The police would be in place, including Trevor and Fraser who would be hidden inside the warehouse where they would be able to reach her quickly when things started to happen.

We had quite a debate about whether I should tell Rob and Melissa about the plan. The decision was to tell Melissa so that she wouldn't agree to baby-sit for Peters or do something to blow the operation. But as for Rob, there was really no reason to involve him.

* * *

The next night we all gathered around the phone while Gabby made the call. She was very cool and controlled. I'll never see her in quite the same light again. I had no idea she possessed such a talent for deception and blackmail. Those of us who were relegated to the role of spectators were more nervous than she was. We could only listen to her side of the conversation. It went something like this.

"Mr. Peters, this is Melissa. I'm fine thanks. I have something I want to talk to you about. Allison told me what she saw in your garage. I figure it must be worth something to you for me to keep quiet. You don't want me running to the cops do you? Of course, you know what I'm talking about. What about that warehouse you've got downtown? Yeah, I know about that too. Allison and I followed you once, and I know exactly what you're up to. The only thing I haven't quite figured out is what you did to Allison. Did you go with her to Elk Lake or did you get someone else to do your dirty work?"

He must have really jumped at that, because Gabby held the phone away from her ear. I could hear him yelling but couldn't make out the words.

"Calm down, that kind of language won't get you anywhere. I think we should meet. Put $50,000 in a duffel bag and meet me tomorrow night at eleven at the warehouse. And come alone. Don't try anything stupid. I'm going to leave a note with all the information I have with someone I trust, and if I don't turn up after our little meeting, she's going straight to the cops. Got that?"

Gabby was acting real tough, but also silly, like I imagined Melissa would. She hung up and collapsed onto the sofa.

"What did he say?" asked Trevor.

"He tried to deny everything at first, but then he agreed to meet me at eleven o'clock tomorrow night. We have to get into the warehouse first and make sure the lights don't work, otherwise he'll recognize right away that I'm not Melissa. It might have been better to pretend to be some other friend of Allison's, someone he's never met."

"Anyone else and I'm sure he would have written it off as a nuisance call. Melissa has been to his house, so she would have had the opportunity to find out what he's up to. I think this is the best way."

"Hey, I think Bill and I need to be given something to do, other than sitting at home waiting. What about if we are stationed near the warehouse where we can at least watch and make sure no one else tries to interfere?" I asked, hoping that Trevor and the others would agree that we could be an asset to the operation.

"I don't know, Sam, you have a knack for getting into trouble. I think I'd feel safer with you several miles away," Trevor joked.

I did not find him the least bit funny. "No way. I want to be close to where the action is, just in case you need my help. I'm going to park the van down the street from the warehouse, just for my own peace of mind."

"Oh, all right. Bill, you can go with the detectives. You'll be stationed outside the warehouse, but ready to assist if we call for you."

Once we had all the details ironed out, everyone went home, agreeing to meet back at our place at eight o'clock the following night. After they left, I asked Gabby one final time.

"Are you sure you want to do this? It could be dangerous."

"I can handle it. It's not going to be any more dangerous for me than it would have been for you. In fact, I venture to say it will probably be a lot less risky. At least I won't do something silly and impulsive," she insisted.

"That's a low blow," I protested. But she was right. My tendency to act before thinking would probably not be an asset in this particular situation.

I couldn't decide what I thought Peters would do. I couldn't see him handing the money over without a fight, and what guarantee would he have that Melissa (Gabby) wouldn't come back for more, or decide to tell the police anyway at a later date? I was guessing he would want to get rid of her, just like he may have done with Allison. That was the scary part. What if he acted so quickly that Trevor and Fraser weren't able to protect her? I shuddered.

"Gabby, I'm scared."

"Not you—Sam—the great thrill seeker? Where's your spirit of adventure?" She laughed nervously. "Now you know how the rest of us feel when you're out running around like an idiot, putting yourself in danger. It's time you had a dose of your own medicine."

We put the dogs outside for a run, cleaned up the coffee cups, and then went upstairs to bed. I crawled in my bed and curled up in a ball. My stomach felt hollow and churned dangerously. What had I gotten us into?

The next day I went to the office and kept occupied with busy work. Each of us was dealing with the tension in his or her own way. Gabby was strangely serene. She had called an emergency meeting of the Psychic Circle, and was planning to meditate at four o'clock, to prepare herself for her role in the operation. I had thought I would be able to use my nervous energy to write a few more pages on my book, but each time I sat down at the computer, I kept seeing Gabby and Peters alone in the warehouse, and me too far away to help. I didn't like this picture at all. The more I thought about it, the more I knew that this scenario would not work for me.

Somehow we all got through the day. When I went home, I caught the tail end of the Circle's meditation. Gabby greeted me at the door, looking calm and relaxed, a far cry from what I felt. After numerous cups of coffee my nerves were jangling.

Everyone turned up at eight as scheduled. We did a dry run of the plan until everyone felt confident that they knew what they were supposed to be doing later that night. Gabby went upstairs to get dressed, having been given a bullet-proof vest to put under her clothes. That gave me a little relief, but not much. It only covered her back and chest. What about the rest?

When she came back downstairs, I was shocked. She had dressed in black and had applied makeup liberally, just like Melissa did. They could have been sisters. Her getup would be good enough to fool Peters at a distance.

At nine, Trevor and Fraser left to go and break into the warehouse. At ten, they called and told Gabby to make sure her rendezvous with Peters took place just outside the office; they were hidden close by, and would be able to hear every word and to get to her quickly if she called for help. They said there was no sign of Peters yet.

As soon as we took their call, Bill and the detectives left in an unmarked police car. Gabby and I were supposed to leave the house about ten-forty. We waited the last few minutes, then, with Clem and Mimi for moral support, headed to the warehouse in the van. The plan was that Gabby would walk the last block and tell Peters she had a friend waiting for her who was going to pick her up at an appointed time. If she didn't show up, the person would drive straight to the police station.

The police had given Gabby a cell phone. Ours was in the van. She had promised to call if things got out of hand. Bill and the police officers would monitor any calls. We thought we had every avenue covered. But then, people always think they've thought of everything. So why do so many well-laid plans disintegrate at the last minute?

What if Peters didn't react the way we thought? He might just pull out a gun and shoot her. Or he might bring someone with him—like that big ape of a truck driver. Someone who could squeeze the life out of Gabby in an instant. A cold chill made it's way down my spine, stopping in the region of my stomach to stir up the butterflies and get them hopping mad.

I drove slowly to the warehouse, dreading every moment. Gabby sat beside me, Clem and Mimi were stretched out in the back. Every couple of blocks, Clem would get up and pace in a circle, coming to lick Gabby's hand before sitting down again. She knew something was up.

We drove slowly down First Street and I stopped the van at the side of the road. Gabby's cell phone rang and I almost jumped out of my skin.

"Hello. Okay, I'll be there shortly, we're about a block away."

"Who was that?" I asked.

"Who do you think, silly. It was Trevor. He says Peters just arrived. He says to get there as quickly as possible. So this is it, I guess. Now, don't do anything stupid, Sam. For once do as you're told. I'll be fine."

"Right," I said glumly. She jumped out of the van before I could grab her and keep her from leaving.

"See you shortly," she called over her shoulder. "Clem, look after Sam."

There was dead silence after she left. I watched her walk quickly to the door of the warehouse and disappear inside. The dogs were restless, but not half as jumpy as me. I craned my neck in the direction of the warehouse. From where I was, I couldn't see where Bill and the detectives were parked. I couldn't see anything. I had to get closer, so I could at least follow the action.

I jumped out of the van and walked quickly toward the warehouse, glad I was dressed in dark clothing too.

At least I would not be easily visible. My plan, if you can call it that, was to get close enough to peer in a window or at least to hear the voices from inside the warehouse. From my previous visit, I knew the layout of the area and remembered a fire escape at the back of the building. From there, I might be able to see inside.

As I turned the corner, I spotted the unmarked police car positioned about a half block from the entrance to the warehouse. They couldn't see me.

There was the fire escape, just where I remembered it. Hoisting myself up to the first step, I climbed quickly to the landing. There was a window in the door, but it was dirty inside and out. I used my jacket sleeve to wipe off the outside which allowed me to peer inside and make out the dark interior.

Suddenly my cell phone, which I had tucked inside my jacket, jangled loudly. I nearly jumped out of my skin, but managed to get it out and push the talk button before it rang again.

"Gabby?"

"No, it's Melissa."

"Gabby, is that you? Just say yes if it's you and you need help."

"Sam, I said it's Melissa. You told me to call you any time, if I needed help. Sam, I'm sorry—"

"Melissa," I whispered urgently into the mouthpiece, "where are you?"

"I'm at home. Mr. Peters called here. My mom answered the phone. He asked to speak to me, and when I went to the phone and said hello, he hung up."

"Oh, no, that means he knows that Gabby isn't you."

"I'm afraid. What's going on?"

"Melissa, don't go out. Don't do anything. I have to go. Gabby's in trouble."

"But Sam, I have to tell you something—"

I hung up. Whatever else she had to tell me would have to wait. I had to let Bill and the others know Gabby was in terrible danger. I scrambled down from the fire escape and took off at a run, around the side of the building and smack into something hard and solid.

"You! May I ask what you're doing here, Ms. Hope?"

The last person I expected to see standing in front of me, a gun pointed directly at my heart, was Darren Gillespie.

"What are you doing here?" I stammered.

"Never mind. Let's go," he said abruptly.

"Where are we going?"

I tried to stall for time, but he jabbed me in the ribs with the barrel of the gun so I decided not to argue. I turned and walked in the direction he was pointing—toward the front entrance of the warehouse. Our little ramble would take us right past the unmarked police car, with Bill and the detectives, hopefully out of sight, inside. I hoped they'd see us and come to my rescue. There it was, just up ahead.

Gillespie hesitated when he saw the car, then seeing no one, walked past the car and pushed me toward the partially open door of the warehouse.

He motioned for me to stop. From where we were

we could see the office. Gabby and Peters were standing in front of it. It was dark but with a little light from the moon shining through one of the dirty windows high off the ground, we could make out their silhouettes. They were talking. He had a duffel bag sitting at his feet. The light glinted off a gun that was tucked in the waistband of his jeans.

Gillespie pushed me with the barrel of his gun and I stumbled forward, accidentally scraping my shoe across the uneven cement floor. The noise startled Gabby who turned quickly. Even in the shadows, I could see her fear.

"Sam, Peters knows who I am."

"I know, don't say anything," I said urgently.

"It's too late for that. I know all about your little scheme," Peters said, giving a nervous laugh. "The real Melissa is safe at home tonight. I'll take care of her later. Right now, we have to get you two out of the way."

"Make that three," Gillespie said, frowning disapprovingly at Peters. "Give me your gun, Peters. Just drop it to the floor very carefully."

Peters did as he was told.

"You've bungled this operation from day one. If it weren't for your incompetence my daughter would still be alive. First you let her find out about the drugs. Now there are two more people here who know too much and will have to be eliminated. I can't let you get away with this. You're going to blow the whole operation."

"What do you mean?" There was a note of panic in

Peters's voice. "You can trust me. I'll take care of everything."

"Sorry, Peters, but you've outlived your usefulness. We're going to have to part company. Permanently. I have millions invested in my little operation, and I'm not going to let you spoil it."

"What are you going to do?"

"I'm not sure." He appeared to study the question for a moment, then answered matter of factly. "But I think that first, I'll get rid of these two busybodies. Then, I'll take care of you."

"I don't think that will work, Mr. Gillespie," a voice called out from the warehouse entrance. "There are other people who know what you're up to."

Who the heck was that? I turned to look, hoping that Bill and the detectives had arrived to save us. My heart stopped as I realized it was Rob standing in the doorway. How did he find out we were here?

"Robert, I should have known Allison would have blabbed to you. That girl never could keep a secret. You're wondering how I know who you are. I read Allison's diary. She wrote reams about you. If I had more time, I would have some very pointed questions about your behavior. But now's not the time for that. Come in and join the party. Now, is there anyone else I should be concerned about?" He looked around quickly.

The silence in the warehouse was palpable. Why had Trevor and Fraser done nothing to help us? Where were our knights in shining armor when we needed them? Were they still hidden close by, listening to everything? Or had Peters or Gillespie found them and put them out of commission? They had to be there behind the shadowy boxes. I glanced around trying to see if I could spot them. It was too dark to make out anything but bulky shapes and large pallets of goods lined up in rows around the warehouse. They could be almost anywhere. Why weren't they breaking up this little party?

Gillespie made us all line up in a row; Peters first, then Rob then Gabby and lastly me. We had our backs to the office, and were facing the still partially open door of the warehouse.

Suddenly I spotted movement near the door. Trying not to change my expression or show any interest was the hardest thing I had ever done. I could just barely make out Bill and the two detectives positioning themselves inside the open door. At last!

Gillespie started. He had heard something and turned quickly, his gun swinging to point at the officers who, illuminated by moonlight, were sneaking through the door. He pulled the trigger.

I grabbed Gabby and knocked her to the ground. As she fell she bumped into Rob who staggered and fell on top of her. Two more shots rang out. Gillespie keeled over, the gun jumping from his hand and skittering across the floor toward me. I picked it up and trained it on Peters who was looking around as though he wanted to make a break for it.

"Not so fast, Peters. You'd better put your hands up, *now*."

His hands went up as he turned toward me.

"We'll take over Sam," Bill said. He and the two detectives had advanced into the warehouse, stopping only to check and see if Gillespie was still alive. He wasn't. They cuffed Peters and left him lying face down on the cement.

"Where the heck are Trevor and Fraser?"

A muffled sound emanated from behind the first row of pallets. Bill headed toward the noise, gun still cocked. Then he started laughing, the kind of high-pitched laugh that comes involuntarily under stress. Now that the worst was over, he could afford to be amused.

"Lot of help you two were."

Trevor and Fraser were tied up, back to back, lying on the ground. Bill untied and helped them get up. They rubbed their hands to get the circulation going as they endured his good-natured teasing.

"Peters seemed to know this was a setup right from the time I arrived," Gabby said.

"Guess who got a call from him about the time he was supposed to be meeting you here?" I asked.

"Not Melissa?" Gabby asked, as it dawned on her why our plan had gone awry.

"You win the grand prize," I joked feebly. My knees were still knocking, and my heart thumping like a hard rock drummer on a bad acid trip.

"Let's get out of here and leave the messy cleanup to those who are paid to do it."

Suddenly I remembered Rob, who was still sitting on the floor, dazed and watching the police go about their business, listening as the sirens got louder and louder. Someone threw a tarp over the body of Gillespie who was lying still on the cold cement.

"Come on Rob, I'll take you home. What the heck brought *you* here tonight?"

"Peters called me, and offered me money if I would keep quiet about the drugs. I came here to try and find out what he had to do with Allison's death. I didn't know about your plan."

"Wait till I tell your mother."

"Don't do that, she'll ground me for the next three years."

"You deserve it after this stunt."

I relented, as I could see he was scared silly. "Come on, let's go. We'll talk about this tomorrow when we've all had a chance to recover."

"I think I've learned my lesson," I said to no one in particular. No more excitement for me."

"If only we could believe you, Sam. But I know you. As soon as you've had a chance to calm down, you'll be looking for some new trouble to get mixed up in."

"Me? Never!"

Epilogue

We all gathered for a debriefing session at the police station a few nights later. All the main players were there. Each told their part of the story so we could fit all the pieces together.

Apparently Gillespie had been the head of an extensive international drug operation. He had hired Peters to handle distribution of drugs arriving from Hong Kong and South America. Gillespie was responsible for a large percentage of the drugs arriving in containers on the West Coast. Peters used unsuspecting locals to unload and load the pallets of drugs as they came in and out of the warehouse. Other than the ape man, better known as Jim Dennison, who was a two-bit thug and known to police, no one was aware of what was really inside the boxes on the pallets.

Trevor and Fraser arrested Dennison after Peters cut a deal to reduce the charges he faced. Dennison told them that when Peters realized Allison knew about the drug operation, he had told Dennison they had to get rid of her.

Peters had called Allison and asked her to baby-sit the night she died. He and his wife had gone out, leaving her with their son. When they came home, Dennison was with them.

When they arrived at the house, they had offered Allison a drink. They had sat and visited with her, giving her a couple more drinks to relax her and make her more susceptible. After a while, Dennison offered to take her home, and she agreed. Instead of taking her home, he had driven in the direction of Elk Lake. When she realized they were going the wrong way, Allison had begun to panic.

When Dennison pulled into the parking area, she had jumped out of the car and tried to run away. He had followed her along the path beside the lake. She had stumbled and fallen into the water. She couldn't swim. He had watched her drown.

Allison had not told Melissa anything about what she had seen in the Peters garage, but she *had* talked to Rob. When she turned up dead, Rob had panicked and convinced his parents to send him to his aunt and uncle's in Nanaimo. Later, thinking things had cooled off and not knowing anyone was aware that he knew what Allison knew, he had come home. He had been afraid to tell Sam or anyone else about what Allison had told him for fear he would be the next victim. The night of the police operation, he had received a call from Peters, telling him to come to the warehouse, and offering him money to shut him up. Foolishly, Rob had agreed to meet Peters. He had called Melissa to let her know he was meeting Peters. She, in turn, had called me on the cell phone. That was what her frantic call had been about. Before she could tell me about Rob, I had hung up in my haste to go to Gabby's aid.

When Peters got to the warehouse, he already knew that someone else would be standing in for Melissa. He planned to deal with whoever it was and then take care of her later. He got to the warehouse early, caught Trevor and Fraser in the act of breaking in, and tied them up. He forced them to call and tell us everything was okay and for Gabby to come to the warehouse.

Gabby walked right into his trap. What Peters didn't know was that Gillespie apparently had plans of his own. It seems he had come to the warehouse expecting to find him there alone. Instead he found me outside and Gabby and Peters inside.

It turned out Judy Gillespie was completely unaware of her husband's drug dealings. When the police visited her to tell her of his death, she broke down completely and had to be hospitalized. Ethel Beauchamp was a real trooper. She had been at Judy's bedside constantly, helping her cope with her double loss.

For Gabby and I, life returned to normal. I made a big decision. As much as I liked the idea of Hope & Henry, P.I.s, I decided to leave the sleuthing to Bill and concentrate on my writing. Out of this little escapade I had the beginnings of a great plot for my next mystery.